Artists

Short Stories

By

Sean De Siun

fiction

Published January 2021
by Art Camino Fiction.

Artists is a series of four short stories.

This book is a work of fiction any resemblance to events or
people past or present is absolutely amazing, but is wholly
a product of the author's imagination.

A CIP record for this book is available
from National LIbrary of Australia

ISBN 978-0-6451139-1-4

COPY SALES
Artists is available on **amazon.com**
Purchase direct from **artcamino.com/fiction**

Distribution enquiries:
Art Camino Fiction

sales@artcamino.com

No.1

The Director

1

Kieran and Cheryl walked arm in arm along Killiney Strand. As it was June, the evening twilight lingered with tinges of red in the swirling high clouds and dappled blue-green waves flopped on the pebbly beach.

'Darling, I'd much prefer it if you came to London with me tomorrow. London is fantastic in the summer and there will be parties and people to meet,' said Cheryl.

'Ah no Cheryl, this summer I need seclusion. I will do as I've planned and go to West Cork. I've not had a real break for ten years. This is my opportunity to reconnect with nature, my nature. More importantly I have to go over the shooting script in fine detail. I need to know it back to front and I have to liaise with Zak. I can't have any distractions.'

'So you will miss the London summer? I bet you won't last three weeks.'

'You know Josh has offered me his house at Inisheen and "I shall have some peace there. For peace comes dropping slow".'

'Really Kieran, you in the countryside, all secluded? What will you do except go mad? I am sure you'll find a local girl, or more likely a backpacker from Sweden to flirt with. I cannot imagine you all alone in boring peace.'

'It's peace I must have now. Besides, I do have to work. Zak will be in Bantry. You know we start shooting in September.'

'Months of work with our wedding in December, no honeymoon. You should come to London with me. It will be our last chance for us to be together for ages.'

'But Cheryl, you'll be working in London. At night you'll be going to parties, drinking, eating. That is exactly what I don't need at this time - distractions. I must prepare myself physically and mentally.'

'Ha, as I said, you'll find someone there to distract you without me there to look after you!'

'Don't be like that, darling. We'll have plenty of time together soon enough. You must concentrate on your work and don't have too much fun. A stint at the National Gallery will do your career a world of good. When the shoot is over, we'll be together full-time.'

'You won't make it through the summer. I'll tell everyone you're coming to London later. But you go and do your Buddha thing.'

'Are you sure you want me in London with you? Maybe you'll enjoy your time without me. When we're married you won't be able to get rid of me at all. "Whenever you look up I'll be there, and whenever I look up you'll be there".'

'Kieran, I love you, but don't try to scare me off. Maybe you are right, absence makes the heart grow fonder. But you'll miss a great summer all the same.'

They reached the north end of the beach and climbed the steps up to the crossing over the train tracks and into Vico Road.

Kieran was fortunate that his work brought him into contact with the glitterati of the Irish film and entertainment industry. Well, glitterati in Ireland, not necessarily Irish. Ireland was a prime film location for big film productions. Big stars, producers and directors had houses on the Southside of Dublin near Killiney.

His friend Josh Blinden was a Hollywood producer and had rented a big place on Vico Road. On a previous trip to Ireland he had bought a 'small get-away' in West Cork. Josh now offered him the house for the summer. One other mutual friend, a painter called Henry, would be going down as well, but probably not for a few weeks.

Kieran and Cheryl walked up to the imposing gates of the house and the security guard waved them in. Josh was having evening drinks on the lawn.

They mingled with a small crowd of people in the industry and sipped champagne as the red sky finally turned dark blue, with the Sugarloaf Mountain turning to a dark silhouette at the south of Killiney Bay past the town of Bray.

It was Friday evening and, as Keiran and Cheryl often did, they wandered down Vico Road after the party to Sorrento Road and into

Dalkey to eat at their favourite Italian restaurant. After dinner they had a drink in the Dalkey Duck.

'Let's go over to Liam's. He's having a session tonight,' said Kieran. They took a taxi to Liam's place in Ballybrack. The door was unlocked and they climbed the stairs to his flat. Inside, musicians sat in a semicircle with others dotted around with various instruments from fiddles to ukuleles, a saxophone and guitars.

The crowded, smoky room was abuzz with lively conversations and laughter. Soon one musician picked up a guitar and began to play, then another joined in and then another. Liam sang and played his guitar until the whole room was playing a part. Kieran shook a tambourine and Cheryl banged a bongo drum.

In the early hours of the morning, Kieran and Cheryl finally pulled themselves away as the session continued, and walked the short distance to their flat in Shankill. Thus ended a typical weekend night for them in South Dublin.

The next day Kieran put his suitcase on the back seat of his Toyota Corolla and Cheryl's bag in the boot, and drove Cheryl to the airport. After they kissed goodbye he continued down the M7 and M8 to Cork City and then he took the N71 through Bandon, Clonakilty and Rosscarbery. As he entered West Cork he deliberately slowed the car down. I had better get into West Cork time, he thought. Down here the time is always 'about half-past'.

He admired the rugged but lush green hills dotted with purple heather and yellow gorse as he slowly drove through Skibbereen to Ballydehob. He continued on down Mizen Peninsula, the most southerly of the five peninsulas that finger out into the North Atlantic. After leaving the town of Schull he caught a glimpse of the Fastnet Rock with its distinctive lighthouse far off the coast, alone, surrounded by sea.

He opened his window to take in the country smell as the car brushed by thick hedges of flowering fuchsia. When he reached Goleen, he stopped and went into the pub to ask directions as Josh had advised him to do. The road to the house at Inisheen, Goleen, near Skibbereen was very secluded, he had been told.

Sometime later the publican came out to the street followed by Kieran and waved his arms pointing up the hill, then down the hill, gesticulating and speaking quickly in a West Cork accent that Kieran could hardly understand at all.

'Many thanks, I think I'll be grand now sure. I'll be back soon... no I won't be a stranger not at all... sure I will... ah sure grand... and thanks again... I will, I will... fine day it is... grand day for driving yes... God bless... your wife too...'

'I thought I'd never get away,' he muttered to himself as he attempted to decipher the convoluted instructions he'd been given.

After only a few wrong turns he came to a crest in the steep, narrow, unsealed road and there he saw the house – Inisheen. Beautiful aspect, he thought as he looked down into the bowl-shaped depression in the hills. At the bottom stood a large stone house surrounded by fields and dry stone walls. The rocky hills climbed one hundred feet or so in three directions and the road ahead passed over another shallower crest on the southern side and disappeared down towards shimmering water below. Beautiful place. Just what I need. Pity I won't have it to myself. But beggars can't be choosers.

He drove up to the house, went in and started to make himself at home. Six weeks of peace and solitude in this lovely house at the southerly tip of Ireland. Bliss. The first thing to do was to make sure the wifi was connected. Ah, super-fast. That's typical – a better connection in the wilds of the country than in town.

Kieran had been living in a small flat above a convenience store but not for much longer, or so he hoped. He had finally secured a major project after ten years of working his way up in the industry. He had been chosen to be Assistant Director of a major film that was going to be shot in the Wicklow Mountains and at Ardmore Studios in Bray. If it went well, as he was sure it would, maybe one day he would end up in a big house on Vico Road, or in Malibu.

He would be working with the Director Zak Flender who was spending the summer working at a house near Bantry not far from Inisheen. At some point in the next few weeks, Kieran would be summoned to meet with him there. The rest of the time he and Zak would go back and forth on the script with notes and emails. He hoped he would only have to work for an hour or two a day. He wanted to spend the rest of the time relaxing and getting mentally fit.

The next morning he woke up early, before sunrise. He climbed the hill on the eastern side of the road and took in the magnificent view, looking northeast as the first rays of the morning sun shone gently on the islands of Roaring Water Bay. The bay was dotted with islets within a convoluted coastline of green and rocky hills. His eyes followed the sunshine as it bathed the coast and the Fastnet that shone like a pearl in the sea. He turned in a full circle with views all around.

Below the sheer cliffs in front of him was the perfect natural harbour of Crookhaven. He could see the village on the other side of the harbour with three pubs and a few houses. Turning south, he looked towards Mizen Head, the most southerly tip of Ireland. To the west he could see across to the Beara Peninsula and the North Atlantic Ocean beyond. He clambered back down to the house and made breakfast.

I am going to completely change my schedule, he told himself. This is the first time I have seen the sunrise for many years apart from when I am getting home from a night out. Kieran normally slept late and either worked or partied until the early hours of the morning.

He determined that he would drink little, eat less, swim in the sea and rise at dawn every day. I am going to read, not just the script, but books, he said to himself with conviction. The large living room in the middle of the house was lined with bookshelves. He cast his eye across them, Proust, Balzac, Zola. Perfect inspiration for any filmmaker. I'm going to meditate and go to bed at ten.

Pleased with his determination to be good and lead a healthy lifestyle for the summer, he pulled a volume off the shelf and sat down to read. I had better be bloody good, he thought, I cannot afford to stuff this job up or I won't be marrying beautiful Cheryl or moving to Hollywood.

He read and wandered around the house and surrounding fields. By mid-morning he had tired of the book and was about to check his email.

Bang, crack, the front door burst open. Henry fell into the room pulling a large roller bag. 'Hi Kieran, good to see you,' he shouted. 'This is a great place isn't it? Wait a minute. I'll get a bottle from the car.'

Seconds later Henry was back brandishing two bottles of Paddy. 'Time for a drinkie-poo eh Kieran? Two lads down south for the summer. We are gonna have some fun, aren't we!'

'Henry, no, no, no. I came down here to rest and work.'

'This is resting. Relaxing with a bottle of whiskey, the best thing for you.'

Surprised by Henry's sudden appearance, Kieran asked, 'What are you doing here anyway? I thought you weren't arriving for weeks.'

'My wife is working shifts, six nights a week, and she needs some space. There's nothing going on in Dublin and the weather is looking great. So I thought I'd come down early. So come on, relax and have a drink with me.'

'Henry, in Dublin I drink all the time, smoke, carry on. I have to get fit and together. I want peace. No drinking for me.'

'Well, Kieran, if I knew you were gonna be like that I would have gone to Malta or Greece. I'm having a drink anyway. I need one after the drive.'

'I thought you were coming here to paint?'

'I am going to paint – tomorrow, or later in the week maybe. I can't bloody well paint all day can I? I'm also going to go to the pubs in Crookhaven and there are parties planned at some of the houses roundabout. It's going to be a classic West Cork summer. There will be music, champagne and women.'

'No women. Definitely no women, Henry.'

'Well actually, there will be at least one woman. A young woman, in fact, and she's very nice indeed I understand. Josh called me last night. He met a girl in Dublin, you know, they had a thing. He said she could stay here and we wouldn't mind at all.'

'When is she arriving?'

'Tomorrow, I think.'

'Good God. My summer is ruined. You know I have no will power. I had to get away or I would be a wreck by the time we start production.'

2

Keiran awoke as the first rays of the sun shone through the window of his bedroom. Oh, the second day and I have already broken my vow to watch the sunrise. He clambered out of bed and sat in the alcove of his window. The house was built in the pre-famine Irish style of dry stone walls nearly a metre thick with stucco on the outside. The window made a wide bench to sit on and look out to the heather, gorse and rugged rocky terrain.

I'll see the sunrise – or nearly! He rushed up the cliffs and turned full circle as the newly-risen sun bathed the landscape in golden rays. Clouds over the ocean to the west danced towards the Irish coastline but looked friendly and benign in the warm summer air. It's going to be a lovely day, he thought and smiled to himself. Now, I must get to work on the script.

He once again clambered down the cliff and made porridge and stewed apple for breakfast with lashings of hot lovely tea. After breakfast, he opened his laptop on the dining table and checked his email.

Subject: Where Are You?

Damn it Kieran I have been up for two hours sending you notes on the script. Where the hell are you? Get back to me soonest.

Zak

Shite, the bastard is either on drugs or winding me up. He hurriedly replied to the email.

Zak, I'm on deck now, sorry to be late. Reading your notes now.

K

He hurriedly read through the seven emails from Zak containing numerous changes, observations and questions about the first page of the script.

Two hours later after frantically working through his responses, he stopped to make himself a jug of coffee.

'Top of the morning, Kieran,' Henry shouted, striding into the kitchen from his bedroom in a loosely fitting dressing gown.

'Henry, do your gown up, will you? I am seeing much more of you than I ever want to again,' said Kieran averting his eyes from Henry's hairy legs and chest.

'Oh sorry, Kieran. I forgot how sensitive you are. I should have remembered from when we were at college.'

Henry strode up to the kitchen counter and turned on the radio.

dum da la dum dum dum… RTE News … The Taoiseach has announced sweeping new reforms to school crossing zones across Ireland …

Henry then grabbed the TV remote and switched it on.

da da de de da da… BBC News … The British Prime Minister today released a plan for sweeping reforms …

'HENRY, turn that bloody racket off NOW!' bellowed Kieran.

'Wha's up wit yas, Kieran? I'm just making me breakfast. Bad hair day, is it?'

'Henry, I was here first. I'm here for peace, so I can work. Don't mess with me, man. You are here to paint. So go and paint. From now on I don't want to see you or hear you or drink with you.'

'Well all right, if that's the way you want it, you tight arsed bastard.'

Aggrieved, Henry tightened his gown, unplugged the radio, nestled it under his arm, raised his nose and marched back to his room.

Kieran opened the back door and went into the garden. He sat at the table and collapsed his head in his arms. What an enervating start to the day. Now I must meditate. He forced himself upright, closed is eyes and his mantra began.

Effortlessly his mantra sprang, again, again, no effort, not trying to think, no thought. Finally, he felt relaxation, a serenity came over him. He felt detached from his fiance, from Zak, Henry. Now he felt he could be productive and work.

'Hello, am I disturbing you?' said a sweet voice.

He opened his eyes to see an auburn-haired girl smiling at him. She was lovely, youthful with vibrant eyes and a gentle smile.

'Are you a vision?'

'Hardly, I'm your housemate, Kayley.'

'Hello, Kayley. A delight to see you nice and early in the morning.'

'What are you doing here sitting all alone?'

'I'm meditating, contemplating the cosmos, you understand – getting ready for the day ahead.'

She was tall with pale green eyes and pouty lips. She looked at him as if he were a source of amusement. She had mischief in her eye, or so he perceived.

'Well, I've just driven up from Cork City. Do you mind if I make myself a cup of tea?' she said and strode off into the kitchen. Kieran followed her. She was beautiful, but he was annoyed at her presence, disturbing his desired peace.

'You came from the city today, Kayley?'

'Yes, from my parents home. I was there for a few days. It's summer holidays now so I can relax a bit.'

'Are you working or studying?' Kieran asked.

'I just graduated from UCD. I hope I'll get a job in September.'

'Ah, what subjects?'

'English, Drama and Film.'

'Very good, the same course as I took when I was your age,' said Kieran.

Kayley smiled at him, 'So you were my age once?'

'Never I was. I mean I went to UCD as well. But I'm here to work. So, although the three of us are here together, perhaps we can agree to keep apart. So I can work, you know. I must have peace and solitude, so please don't be offended if I rather ignore your presence.'

'You must have very important work to do?'

'It's important to me.'

'Really? What are you up to down here in West Cork?'

'I'm reviewing the script of a movie that we're shooting in September.'

'Is that right? Well, I shall try my best to leave you to it.'

Kayley turned away and opened the kitchen cupboards to see what each one contained. She found a bowl and poured muesli into it.

'Well I'll see you around I guess ... what's your name, anyway?'

'Me? I'm Kieran.'

'Nice to meet you Kieran, I suppose,' said Kayley as she turned her back on him again and strode out into the garden.

Kieran followed her into the sunshine. The kitchen faced west and puffy white clouds danced overhead, dappling sunshine and shadow on the hills and crags.

'Where is my bedroom?' she asked.

'Come, I'll show you and you can choose.'

The original stone building had two rooms on the ground floor and two rooms above. But Josh had greatly extended the house, adding new rooms to each side. It now had five large bedrooms, each with an en suite bathroom.

'This is my room,' said Kieran as he waved at a closed door at the top of the stairs. This room is Henry's where he is sulking after I was mean to him, and there are three more bedrooms down the corridor. Take your pick.'

'I think I'll take the one that is furthest away from your room,' said Kayley.

'Very sensible, but I'm more worried about you biting me than you should be worried about me biting you,' said Kieran.

3

Kieran left Kayley to settle into her room and went downstairs into the open plan living and dining room where he had set up his computer to work. He heard creaking from Henrys' car boot and a dragging sound.

Henry set up his easel in the garden and began to paint. Kayley joined him and they talked and laughed. Keiran became fascinated by Kayley. She was so self-confident. As she chatted with Henry she didn't seem overbearing or shy. She was serene, mature.

I've got to get away from them, he told himself. I must keep on the straight and narrow. He put on his swimming trunks, picked up a towel and left them to it, driving to the beach at Barleycove for a swim.

I'm just going to ignore them both assiduously, pretend they are not there. My life is going to change one way or the other. I won't be going back to the 'scene' in Dublin, that's for sure.

The wide sandy beach was nearly deserted when he arrived. He splashed in the surf for as long as he could stand the cold water. The sun sparkled through the dappled clouds. The breeze coming from the south was warm. The salty ocean smell reminded him of being with Cheryl walking along Killiney Beach.

He sat on the sand for a while and then decided to head back to the house to do some work. As his car turned into the narrow driveway, a car pulled out and nearly hit him.

'Sorry!' the young male driver shouted as he reversed the car back so that Kieran could drive in. Kayley was on the front seat next to him, laughing. As soon as he was in the driveway the car sped away tooting twice on its way out. Kayley waved her hand out the window at Kieran.

Henry was still painting in the garden out the back. Although he had decided to ignore his two housemates, Kieran was curious. He went into the garden, and asked, 'Henry, who was that?'

'I don't know, Kieran. Some fella arrived and beeped his horn. The next thing, Kayley was running out the door.'

'Did you talk to her much?'

'We did have a nice conversation indeed.'

'What do you make of her?'

'Agh, she's just a young woman out for a good time. What do you expect?'

'Nothing, I guess. She's good looking all right.'

'Not bad at all, very pretty. You're not thinking of having a go are you?'

'No no not at all. I have to work, as I keep saying. Straight as an arrow I must be.'

'Come off it, Kieran. What's with all this Mr Serious stuff? It's not like you at all. You're the life and soul of the party.'

'Not now Henry. I have an opportunity here. I'm going to change my life. I'll be successful.'

'Well, you've lined up your trophy wife and landed this job. But that doesn't change who you are. They'll see through you eventually.'

'Stop, Henry. We're not so young any more. You think of me as the wild youth. I'm growing up, maturing.'

'Ha, rather ripening like an old cheese! Have you finished work for the day?'

'I guess so, there's nothing more I can do until Zak fires off a million questions for me at four in the bloody morning. I thought I would be very quiet and read through the script.'

'Come on, don't be silly. I can see you need to shake off some of your fear. You seem very nervous, Kieran. I'll drive – let's go to Crookhaven for a pint.'

Kieran gave in. It was true that there was nothing much he could do until he received more instructions from Zak. But one little drink will be all right, he told himself. I'll start work in earnest tomorrow.

As Henry's car passed over the top of the hill and down the steep road to the coast below, the Fastnet shone like a jewel in the sea. Crookhaven was a deep and narrow inlet. The village of Crookhaven consisted of three pubs around a square with the harbour on the fourth side, a few houses and a church. There was a stone harbour wall for small fishing boats and a fisherman's co-op.

Henry parked the car and they went into O'Sullivan's Bar. A slogan painted on the wall outside read 'The Most Southerly Pint in Ireland'.

'Two pints of Murphy's, please', said Henry.

They took their drinks outside and sat at a table overlooking the harbour. 'See across the way, Kieran. On the top of that cliff. That's where Inisheen is.'

On the mainland side of the inlet was a sheer rock bluff about 300 ft tall. At the base was a buttress and old constructions.

'What is that, Henry?'

'It's an old copper mine. Marconi made the first-ever radio broadcast across the Atlantic from here. He chose this location because he needed copper to make his radio transmitter.'

'Well, there you are Henry, a mine of information.'

'My family used to come down here for the summer when I was a kid. We stayed at Barleycove. It's a beautiful spot. We came here to Crookhaven to buy mackerel, straight off the fishing boats. You never tasted better fish in your life. Sláinte,' he said, lifting his pint of stout to his mouth.

They sipped their beers and admired the view. Two beers later, the sun was getting low in the sky. But it was mid-June and summer solstice was just a few days away, so it would not get dark until after 10 pm. They relaxed as the long twilight unfolded.

More people came for a drink, and by the early evening it was quite lively. A session started up and Irish music wafted out from the pub opposite O'Sullivan's.

'Cheers Kieran, hic, it's great to see you again. It's been a while since we tied one on together.'

'Too long all right, Henry.'

'Tell me, Kieran. How did you land this job anyway? The last time we talked you were Assistant Director of Photography.'

'In truth Henry, it was a bit of a try on, a confidence trick. That is, I gave them confidence in me, misplaced confidence. I was working on the final series of 'Return of the Viking'. The director needed someone to look after the second unit that was shooting extra scenes up at Powerscourt and in the Wicklow Mountains. I made up a story that I had directed a prize-winning short film and got the gig. To my amazement when the series came out I was credited as one of two Assistant Directors.

'Then I was approached by Zak Flender's people who were looking for an Assistant Director for this show.'

'What is the movie you are going to make called again?'

'That's the thing that got me the job, Henry. It's called 'Vikings: Zombies Awake'.'

'Zombie Vikings. You're kidding?'

'Not at all. I'm sure it's going to be a smash hit. Because of my credit on 'Return of the Viking' and experience shooting in Ireland and Wicklow, they thought I might be suitable. The other assistant director who had worked on Vikings wasn't available so they called me. However, Zak wanted to hear my ideas and see if I would be able to work with the Director of Photography and the rest of the team. That's where the auld charm came in.

'I read everything I could about Zak, the DP and everyone else involved with the project and I constructed a story that made it seem that my ideas jelled with theirs perfectly.'

'Good man, well done. Do your ideas jell with theirs?'

'I don't have any ideas at all. I never had it mind that I would direct. Sure, I hoped to be DP one day … in a few years maybe. But they gave me the job and I've been running to catch up ever since. I don't have much confidence that I can pull this off.'

'Go 'way, Kieran. You'll be fine, no worries at all. If you can bluster your way into a position like this it demonstrates that you are capable.'

'We'll see. Assistant Director is possibly the worst job there is. I'll get the blame for every stuff-up. If takes are not up to scratch, it will be down to me. If we don't meet our deliverables schedule, my fault. If the movie is a success, all the credit will go to Zak.'

'Well drink up old boy, leave your troubles at the bar. The night is young. Let's go inside and see who's around.'

By now the whole village had turned into one big pub party. Customers from the three bars strolled from one to the other. It was like one establishment with an outside area. It was a beautiful evening and the sky turned orange, then an ever-deepening blue until well after 10 o'clock when the stars finally came out.

Laughing, joking and singing, it was like a family get-together. Everyone acted as if they had known each other for years, even if they had never met.

'Hey, long lost friend! What's your name again?'

'Hic, I'm Kieran and this is Henry.'

'That's right,' said the fellow that Kieran had never laid eyes on before. 'How's your father?'

'Ah sure he's grand he is, I'll let him know you were asking for him. What's your name again?'

'Johnny O'Sullivan from Drinagh. This young man here is my cousin Brian. Over there is his brother and sister, and over there are our cousins from Kerry.'

'Is it a family reunion you're having?'

'Not really, it's just that whenever we come to Crookhaven there seem to be a lot of O'Sullivans around.'

Kieran and Henry mingled and drank until after midnight when Henry said, 'Kieran, I'll leave the car here and we can walk home.'

'Walk? It's too far.'

'We'll be all right. It's not as far as it looks, just a few kilometres.'

They stumbled around the coast road and up the hill back to Inisheen. Kieran glanced at the clock as he fell into bed and saw it was 1:30. Oh God, I have to get up in a few hours.

He was sound asleep until woken by loud crashing and doors banging. He heard Kayley laughing and the sound of kissing. Two pairs of feet climbed noisily up the stairs and crashed into Kayley's room. The unmistakable sounds of passionate lovemaking kept Kieran awake. He covered his head with his pillow and drifted back to sleep.

'Kieran, Kieran! Your phone's been ringing repeatedly for an hour. It might be the boss, you had better answer it,' Henry shouted at him.

He opened his eyes and there was Henry once more in his dressing gown with his hairy chest and belly bulging out. 'Oh, my head hurts. What time is it?'

'It's 9:30.'

'Oh no, no, Zak will kill me.'

He pulled himself together and made coffee. He went to his computer on the dining table and checked his email. Sure enough, about a dozen emails had arrived from Zak. The last one read –

I need reliability. If I cannot depend on you to be working when I am, you are no use to me. WHERE ARE YOU?

Er, er, he picked up his phone. 'Hi Zak. Sorry, I had a bit of an emergency, yes, yes I know, er. OK, you're right but you know, an emergency…'

Henry was in the kitchen that opened onto the living room and smiled when he heard Zak bellow,

'I DON'T CARE IF YOU'RE ON A SINKING SHIP. YOU'RE WORKING FOR ME. BE THERE WHEN I NEED YOU GODDAMIT.'

'OK, OK, it won't happen again. I can promise you. I ran out the door to handle an emergency and left my phone behind. In future, no matter what, I will be there whenever you call. I'm onto it now, goodbye.'

A few minutes later Kayley and her boyfriend came downstairs and proceeded to make breakfast, smiling at each other with knowing eyes.

'You don't look too well, Kieran. Were you working all night?' she said with a smirk.

Determined to stay calm and project an air of professionalism, he said, 'Kayley, you are disturbing me. I came here to work and for peace and quiet.'

Henry, Kayley and her friend all burst into laughter. Realising the hopelessness of his situation, he unplugged the power cord from the wall, picked up his computer and mouse and took them to his bedroom. This will have to be my living space from now on, he told himself.

He had taken the master bedroom. It had a large picture windows looking into the back garden and the surrounding hills as well as the alcove that looked out to the driveway.

A short while later he heard two toots of a car horn and the screech of wheels and engine roar. Kayley had gone out with her boyfriend. He spent the rest of the day replying to Zak's emails. At the end of the afternoon, he felt satisfied that he could do no more until the next barrage from Zak. Henry was painting in the garden and he went to the kitchen for something to eat. He was pleased to have a quiet evening and went to bed exactly at 10pm.

He was woken from his sleep once again by a loud noise as Kayley and her friend thumped up the stairs for another sex session. Awake and tormented, he covered his head with his pillow but, as he was sober, it didn't work. He lay awake listening to them until their bed at last stopped creaking. He glanced at his watch – it was 2 am.

His phone alarm woke him at 5:30 and he checked his email before making coffee. Thanks be, no emails from Zak. So he is human after all, he thought. However, an hour later the emails started and Kieran set to work.

Mid-morning, he made some more coffee, went into the garden and sat down across from Henry with his back to the kitchen door.

'Top of the morning to you, Kieran. Fine day, is it not?'

'Fine day it is for sure.'

He felt relaxed. Perhaps this will work out after all. If I can keep Henry at bay and Kayley is either in or out with her boyfriend all the time, I should be able to get through this, he thought.

A few minutes later Kayley came into the garden followed by her boyfriend. Henry looked up and his jaw dropped. Kieran wondered what he was staring at and swivelled around to look. His jaw dropped as well. Kayley was with a different boy this time.

'Good morning, gents,' said Kayley. 'This is my friend, Michael.'

'Good morning, Kayley and Michael,' Henry and Kieran said in unison.

This boy lasted two nights. But on the third morning, he drove off leaving Kayley behind. A few hours later Kieran looked up from his computer to see a new car come into the driveway. A young man stepped out of a Mercedes as Kayley ran out to meet him. She threw her arms around him and they kissed. They got into the car and the Mercedes slowly exited and made its way out of Inisheen.

My God, what an operator she is, he thought. She is a very popular girl. He couldn't work anymore. He was getting used to the torment of listening to her lovemaking. Last night he lay in bed with his eyes wide shut imagining that it was himself in her bed, in her arms, beneath the sheets drinking in her musky scent. With each sigh, he felt it was he that was giving her pleasure. He heard the boy moan and he felt the tingling sensation as if she were caressing him.

Now that there was a third boy, he couldn't stand it. He felt like a tragic Greek character, tortured anew each day. He went to talk to Henry in the garden. 'Did you see that, Henry?'

'She went off with her boyfriend, I guess.'

'Her new boyfriend it was.'

'What a third bloke? She is a tiger, isn't she? Have you heard her making love every night?'

'How could I not hear it? I'm being driven crazy.'

Sure enough that night Kieran was woken again, this time after Kayley and her friend were already in bed. With this boy she was quiet, he could hardly hear them at all. This fellow seemed a bit less boorish than the other two. It made him despise him even more.

Now, he didn't imagine him in his place. No, he pictured himself as the indignant lover discovering his mistress in bed with another man. He would storm through the door and pull him off of her. 'Get out you wretched dog,' he would say and watch the blackguard drive away meekly in his bloody Mercedes, his hands on his hips and a menacing glare in his eyes. It would be best to shoot it day for night, yes, and black and white. Humm, what lens would I need? Then he would seize Kayley and ravish her.

He created a complete scenario. The story ended as he and Kayley left from the harbour at Crookhaven, standing on the back of a fishing boat with the rugged captain in his Aran sweater, pipe in mouth, winking and saying, 'Don't you two lovers worry, we'll reach the coast of France before morning.'

They would embrace as the sun set behind them, a light mist drifting across as the boat pulled slowly away from the camera, fade to black, roll credits. Yes, 'Gone with the Sea', Directed By Kieran Coakley ASC. ... Academy Awards, BAFTA.

His phone rang, twillip, twillip, 'Hello, yes Zak, I am awake ...'

4

Keiran put down his phone and looked over the two pages of notes he had written while talking to Zak.

Well, at least I know what I have to do. He breathed a sigh of relief. No more waiting. He had much to do and his thoughts raced forward to getting on set and out into the Wicklow Mountains to shoot the movie.

He was responsible for all second unit filming. This involved a variety of shots. He would direct the filming of empty backgrounds that the digital versions of the Viking village and actors would be composited into later. He would also direct the crowded battle scenes that did not involve the principal actors. One scene had thousands of zombie Vikings marching up a hill, down another and storming castle walls. Extras would be placed at intervals around a large field with trackers on them, marching back and forth. The VFX crew would then use software to fill in all the gaps with computer-generated characters to give the impression of a multitude of zombies. He was also responsible for many of the secondary green screen shots that would be used with the backgrounds in the final composite.

Zak would concentrate on directing the scenes with the principal actors.

It was very complicated work planning for all the eventualities that might occur. It was too expensive to figure everything out on set with dozens of paid crew standing around. The starring actors would only be available for a specified number of days before flying off to their next show. Every detail had to be worked out before any money was spent on set. A team of people, with Zak at the head, had been working out the complex details for months.

Now all the arrangements were being finalised. After the six week semi holiday in West Cork, Kieran would spend August at Ardmore Studios working with the VFX supervisor before the actors and production crew arrived in September.

Kieran sent his replies to Zak's long list of questions. It was 2 pm and he sat back in his chair and relaxed with the rest of the day to himself.

The front door slammed and he heard Kayley run up the stairs and close her bedroom door. She's home early, he thought. She had been with Mr Mercedes for three nights and they seemed very happy together each morning at breakfast. But she was alone now.

Last night he had managed to sleep without interruption. But now he was grateful for the intrigue that Kayley had brought. Inspired, his wild dream from a few nights before had solidified into a movie idea. He was working on the story in the afternoons when he had finished on Zombie.

It was a romance, of course, set at Crookhaven and surrounds. If Zombie is a hit, who knows, maybe this will go somewhere, he thought.

The first week at Inisheen had not turned out as expected, but he was now feeling settled in.

He looked out the window and saw Henry working on his painting. He went downstairs to join him.

'How's the painting coming along, Henry?'

'Not bad. What do you think?'

Kieran looked over the large canvas. The hills were a red colour and the trees and shrubbery a funny orange and yellow. The stone walls were an otherworldly green, 'Overall, Henry, it is strangely compelling, even beautiful.'

'Thanks, I appreciate that. It is a semi-commission. An art dealer in Dublin said he could sell as many of this type of painting as I could do. I hope to get five grand for this one.'

'Very good. Did you hear Kayley come in? She was alone.'

'Yes, the Mercedes man dropped her off. Could that mean a peaceful night?'

'Maybe, or perhaps there's another fella on the way over right now. How do you think she has the energy not to mention the mental capacity for so many men in her life?'

'Well Kieran, I think she's just young. She's doing what we would do if we had the chance. Never turn an opportunity down, especially not a romantic opportunity.'

'True enough. I've had my share of short term romances. That's all I have ever had, just not so close together.'

'Until now that is, eh? I mean you're engaged to Cheryl.'

'Yes I am engaged. Somehow I haven't thought of Cheryl for days. In fact I'd forgotten all about her.'

'You've been dreaming about Kayley, I bet.'

'Not at all!'

'Well I bloody well have been. Every night, imagining me in her arms. Seriously, Kieran. I can see the way you look at her. You're every bit as interested in her as I am. More than I am – I have my wife waiting at home. I'm in no need of any attachments – not even one night stands.'

'Henry you're wrong, I'm not the slightest bit interested in her. She's not my type at all. Besides she is probably ten years younger than us. Intellectually, physically, emotionally, we're not suited at all.'

'Well, that is pretty definitive all together. If you're not interested, then, I dunno, maybe I am after all.' Henry smiled, looking Kieran directly in the eyes.

Kayley came out of the kitchen hands in the back pockets of her jeans. She looked relaxed, less tense than she had been with her boyfriends. 'Hello fellas, let's see the painting. Humm, interesting use of colour Henry.'

'You're back early, Kayley. Are you going out again?' said Henry.

'No, nothing on tonight. My friend's gone back to Dublin.'

'What about your other friends? Will you be seeing them again?' asked Kieran.

'No, they were just boys I met down here, didn't go anywhere.'

'Too bad,' said Henry, 'But you know what day it is, don't you both? It's summer solstice, midsummer night.'

'So it is. Shall we all dance naked around a campfire?' said Kayley.

'Now you're talking. That's a great idea. But I have a genuine idea for us to celebrate the day,' said Henry.

'What do you have in mind?' said Kieran

'I'll show you some of the sights of this area. We can have a look at a few Celtic monuments and drive down a couple of the peninsulas.'

'Sounds good! Let's go,' said Kayley.

'First stop Mizen Head, the most southerly tip of Ireland.'

Keiran sat in the back and Kayley in the front beside Henry. Kieran already regretted what he had said to Henry. Not interested in her? He was fascinated by her. After all, he was writing a starring role in a film for her character. He looked at Kayley's profile as she turned to talk to Henry.

Great shot, he thought. He planned it all out in his mind. The front windscreen would have scenes of Paris at night with lights flashing as they drove past La Coupole and down the Champs-Élysées. He figured out how to light the inside of the car to make her look like Ingrid Bergman.

Henry drove them all around the Mizen and Sheep's Head Peninsulas. They stopped periodically to take in the beautiful scenes. Henry and Kayley talked animatedly and laughed at each other's jokes. Kieran felt left out and stared out his window as the countryside kaleidoscoped past. He felt like excess baggage being dragged around as he opened his car door and stepped out to look at yet another breathtaking sight. Henry and Kayley had already run to the top of a rocky lookout without even looking to see if Kieran was still there. After a while, they ran back and jumped in the car and Henry started to drive off.

'Hang on, Henry!'

'Oh, sorry, Kieran. I thought you were still in the car.'

Henry drove quickly along the narrow twisting roads. Kayley put her hand on his knee affectionately and Henry glanced knowingly into her eyes.

'Is she really falling for Henry?' Kieran wondered. Deflated, he opened his window to feel the rush of cool, fragrant summer air. A sense of failure filled him, of being left out.

Henry parked the car at a tea shop near the end of the Sheep's Head Peninsula. 'Let's have tea and scones,' said Henry as they stepped out of the car. 'Kieran, you go ahead and order for us. Kayley and I will have a look at the view.'

Kieran ordered a pot of tea for three and chose three slices of cake from the display cabinet.

'That makes 45 Euro,' said the German serving girl. The Italian waiter said, 'Here, a table has just become free, please to sit. You will have a pleasant view of the ocean.'

Soon the waiter brought over the pot of tea. Kieran looked at the ocean waves crash on the cliffs below. A few hundred yards away Henry and Kayley stood on a rock ledge. Henry put his arms around Kayley and they kissed.

You bastard Henry, damn it. Kieran turned his head away. He looked again and they had disappeared. Fifteen minutes later they emerged in the distance clambering over the rocky spine of the peninsula.

They made their way into the cafe and drank a cup of cold tea and ate their cake in silence, looking into each other's eyes oblivious of Kieran.

He felt abandoned, alone, by his own design. He had spurned Kayley, pushed her away from him. Henry had even offered her to him, and now he was left behind.

'Let's go home and spend the evening gazing at the stars,' said Henry to Kayley, his eyes soft like a puppy's, his hand in hers.

Back at the house, Henry pulled a pot-belly stove out of the shed and into the garden.

'I'll make a nice turf fire,' he said to Kayley.

Kieran slunk off to his room with a bottle of whiskey. He looked out of his bedroom window at the two of them, sipping his drink. Kayley and Henry sat gazing at the fire, entwined in each other's arms as the evening twilight slowly turned to a bright star-filled night. The warm glow of the crackling turf shone across their faces. They looked happy, in love.

He woke up with a start, his head in his arms on his desk, the whiskey bottle in front of him nearly empty. He rubbed his face and shook his head. Looking out the window to check on the two love birds, he could only see the soft dying embers glowing in the stove. Henry and Kayley had gone.

'Well, that's that, blown it, disaster,' he cried out as he stumbled onto his bed and crashed asleep.

Despite his hangover, he forced himself out of bed at 7:30. Thankfully, there were no emails from Zak. Maybe he had a mid-summer night party as well, he thought. He was still in his clothes from the day before. He had a shower and went downstairs to make breakfast.

While he was eating his cereal Henry emerged from his room in his dressing gown. He hastily wrapped it around himself more fully and tightened the chord.

'Good day to you, Kieran. If you don't mind I will quietly make some breakfast so as not to disturb your morning meditations.'

'Of course, Henry. Go ahead. How does Kayley like her eggs?'

'I'm only making breakfast for myself.'

'I'm surprised, you two were getting on so well last night.'

'True enough, but she's not ready for another relationship. She says that she respects me. I'll have another go today.'

'Oooh, respect. That's a bad sign. Looks like you're out of the picture, my old boy!'

'As I said, I'll keep at it.'

Kieran felt a wave of relief sweep over him. A smile took over his face. He stretched his arms and picked up his mug of coffee. 'Ah, I feel great today. Nothing from Zak, the weather is beautiful. It's going to be a wonderful day,' he said as he sprang up and took the staircase two steps at a time to get back to work.

There was still nothing from Zak so he started to work on his story. The title had changed from 'Gone With the Sea' to 'From There Through Eternity'. He banged away at his keyboard until lunchtime.

Why am I so relieved that Henry failed to seduce Kayley? I guess it means that she actually does need to be seduced, not just propositioned, he thought.

Intrigued, unable to fathom her, he felt a need to see her that instant. He walked through the house and around the garden looking for her but she wasn't there. Henry was nowhere to be found either. He walked out to the driveway. Henry's car was gone and his heart sank.

5

Kieran sat at his desk in his room all afternoon waiting for Henry and Kayley to return. He could hardly move let alone work. Frozen, numbed, he looked at his computer screen, flitting from website to website.

The Irish Times, nothing to read, the Guardian, nope, the New York Times, same headlines as all the rest, the Telegraph, Express, shock horror probes, scandal, romping royals, insane politicians. It made him feel no better to flick from one news outlet to the next. Like eating junk food, always desiring fulfilment, but never finding it, nevertheless the addict continues to search for satisfaction in the same failed remedies.

He could not look at the script or his new story, nothing until he knew if Henry had succeeded in seducing Kayley. The hours gnawed at his psyche, twisting his thoughts. He felt unable to think, 'How could I have been so stupid?' he wondered.

As afternoon turned into evening his nervousness fell into a dreary resignation. I have missed my chance at happiness. I let my best friend steal the love of my life, he wailed inside.

As dusk set in he had a glass of wine and his mood changed. After the third glass he began to feel a bit more like himself. Oh well, never mind, I didn't really fancy Kayley at all, he rationalised.

At last he worked up enough courage to check his email after a seven-hour hiatus. Sure enough, Zak had sent him five new emails. He immersed himself in the intricate details of how he was going to direct the scene when the female Viking zombies (the un-dead Shield Maidens) were to rape a group of living Irish monks and make it seem realistic.

His mind ablaze, his head full of wine and now whiskey, he tapped frenetically at the keyboard with just one table lamp in the corner of his room to light the darkened house. He pulled at his unshaven chin, and scraped his fingers through his unwashed hair, eyes ablaze as he imagined zombie Valkyries devouring ...

Clunk, the front door shut. He heard two sets of footsteps and murmurs. He strained his ears to listen and he made out the sound of Henry saying, 'Well, there you are then.'

The footsteps clunked up the stairs and diverged at the landing, Henry going to his room and Kayley to hers. Two doors slammed shut.

At last freed from his torment, Kieran downed the last slug of his whiskey and, now satisfied, brushed his teeth, washed his face and went to bed.

He awoke with a terrible headache but checked his email. There was nothing from Zak. He felt sure he must be wearing him down by now. No one could keep up such a pace and expect other people to stay with them. At first Zak terrified him, now he felt he had his measure. Most of his incessant questions were repetitions of Zak's own fears. How will this work, what will the end result look like, will the producers 'give it love'?

As he made his way downstairs the fear and insecurity of the day before clawed its way through his hangover. He made his breakfast as usual, with a dose of two aspirin as an eye-opener.

Henry's door creaked open and he emerged hauling his suitcase. He dragged it down the stairs making a big clunk at each step. When he reached the bottom he looked up at Kieran, tortured.

'I am an artist,' he declared, 'I can no longer work under these oppressive conditions. I must, yes, I have no other recourse but to leave, at once! If I am not wanted I shall take my talents to where others, more knowing, will give me the appreciation my work deserves.' He raised his gaze to the ceiling, chin held out.

Kieran clapped his hands slowly, clap, clap, clap. 'Good performance, Henry.'

'All right ye bastard,' said Henry.

'Come and have heat of the tea,' said Kieran.

Henry made his breakfast and sat down with Kieran. 'I have my dignity intact,' he said. 'She's no lady. Well, she isn't perfect anyway.'

'Did she wrong you in some way, Henry?'

'No, no it's not that. It's just that she is incapable of understanding an artist like me. She is vapid, lifeless. She appreciates nothing of the subtleties of this world. I was wrong to see her in a more favourable light, as if she were more emotionally evolved. No, no, she is not worth the effort for me to educate her.'

'Henry, so what you are saying is that she wouldn't sleep with you?'

'No, of course, it's not that. Not at all. I have no need for sexual fulfilment, but I lust for spiritual enlightenment. That which she is incapable of understanding.'

They looked up as they heard Kayley's door open and her footsteps on the stairs. She came into the kitchen with a serene smile on her face, and a black pair of yoga pants and top.

'Good morning, Kayley. You look like a ninja,' Kieran smiled.

'Morning guys,' she said. 'You both look as if you're expecting something.'

'No Kayley, I have no more expectations of you,' said Henry, his eyes drooped down to the floor.

'Ah sure, don't be like that Henry, you know I respect you. I feel tenderness towards you in my own way and I love your painting,' Kayley said.

'My painting? What do you know of art? You will never grow to understand art, culture. You are too vain to understand the true meaning of art.'

'Now Henry, what way is that to talk to our guest? Don't be so judgemental,' said Kieran.

'You are right, the two of you - ganging up on me as you are. In any case, I have to get back to Dublin immediately. Then I think I'll book a flight to Malta. My brother and his family take a villa there every year at Gozo. It's great fun. Sun, cheap food and booze. You should try Malta some year, said Henry'

Kieran laughed inside and smiled as sweetly as he could, at Kayley. They finished their breakfasts, saying no more.

Henry hauled his bag, painting and easel into his car and drove over the hump down to Crookhaven and the road back to Dublin. Kayley and Kieran waved goodbye.

Now Kieran was left alone with Kayley. She looked sad and without a glance or word turned and strode back into the house and up to her room. Kieran heard her door slam shut and his heart fell.

He climbed the stairs back to his room and worked listlessly, replying to yet more emails from Zak. Zombies, I'm not sure I can relate to this anymore, he thought. I'm more interested in people who are alive.

He turned to his movie treatment, now titled 'The Eternal Sea', and worked on that instead. This title he felt sure captured the feeling of loss and melancholy that he was trying to convey. The sense of love unrequited, the cruelty of nature and the unremitting flow of time, the sea, love and waves.

Kieran gazed out his bedroom window to the west as the afternoon sun smothered the yellow gorse and purple heather with golden rays and dappled shadows. Low cumulus clouds danced across the landscape from west to east. Transfixed by the unfolding skyscape, he sat motionless as the twilight set in and the crimson clouds cast a magical glow across Inisheen.

Kayley at last came out of her room and tiptoed down to the kitchen. Kieran followed in his socks, no shoes, so as not to break the silent mood.

Still dressed in her ninja outfit, Kayley glanced over her shoulder at him.

'Sad are you, Kayley?' asked Kieran.

'Sad? Not at all. Why should I be sad?'

'Er, I dunno, I guess the house has been so quiet all day I felt a bit melancholy, you know, after Henry left like that.'

'Ah, don't worry about Henry, he's fine. Just a bit of a drama queen you know, don't you?

'Do you feel no remorse?'

'Remorse, are you kidding? We had a fun couple of days, messing around. What did you guys expect, that I would leave my husband and run away with him? Oh, that's right, I'm not married, but he is. So you think I'd be a home breaker?'

'I guess he expected more from you. You seemed to like him.'

'Kieran, he was chasing me, not the other way around. It's flattering to have someone show interest in you. Maybe guys don't understand that because they are usually the chasers, not the ones being chased.'

Kieran felt humbled, caught out. It was true that he and Henry had considered her fair game, to be seduced if not hunted. 'You are right, Kayley, we've not shown that much interest in you, in who you are. Only in what you are, which is a fascinating and beautiful woman.'

She smiled at him, 'There you go again, flirtation and flattery.' She laughed and sat down at the kitchen table.

'So what's this important movie you're working on,?'

'It's called 'Vikings: Zombies Awake'.'

'Zombie Vikings? You're pulling me leg aren't ye?'

'Not at all, it's going to be a big hit.'

'Why zombies?'

'Well, zombie films are one of the constants in Hollywood. Ever since 'White Zombie' in 1932 there have been numerous zombie movies, and now is the time for the next one.'

'How do you mean?'

'Studios are always looking years ahead at their release schedules. They go through cycles of genres. You know werewolf, vampire movies. Zombie movies always sell but you can't do them every year. Their data steered them to the conclusion that next year is perfect for the next zombie wave.'

'Sounds like looking into tea leaves.'

'It is, but driven by research, focus groups, group psychology, data, but most importantly, money.'

'Why Vikings?'

"Return of the Viking' was a hit series. It spawned several shows along the same lines. You know, hunky guys chopping off heads and Valkyrie-like women, sex, adventure. It's a perfect dramatic mix.'

'So the data say, next year is Vikings and zombies?'

'Exactly. The only trouble is that often several studios come to the same conclusion at the same time. So there is always a danger that you end up with three movies in a similar genre in the same year. As far as we know, we are the only zombie movie going into production this year. So the road is clear and we are expecting it to be a big hit.'

'As a film school graduate, it seems disappointingly un-artistic to just repeat the same old formulas.'

'Perhaps, but a lot of artistry and craft will go into making the film. Zak Flender has never made a film that didn't make money, and he has two hits under his belt.'

'So it's all about the money?'

'At this level for sure. But art is always driven by money, isn't it? If it weren't for the Catholic Church, there would be no European art history. The same is true for eastern art – religious patronage was the driving force. I mean, they had the resources to pay for artisans, sculptors, painters, draftsmen. Nowadays it's commerce, capital that provides the impetus for artistic endeavours.'

'You sound like one of my lecturers. Perhaps that's what you should do, teach art history.'

'Thanks Kayley. I hope I can still do, not just teach.'

'Oh well, your lecture sent me to sleep. Now I have to go and lie down. I'll have an essay ready for you tomorrow,' said Kayley.

'Don't be like that, Kayley. Stay and we can cook dinner together.'

'Fine. I'll cook my food and you can make yours.'

They began to prepare their evening meals, Kayley on one side of the island counter and Kieran opposite her.

'Who was your friend with the Mercedes?' he asked her.

'He was in my class at uni and we were together for a while. He did his last year at a film school in Germany, so we split up, both agreeing it was best. We're still friends though, nothing serious at all. I just saw him for old times sake.'

'What about the other boys?'

'Ah, just guys I met down here. Friends of friends. Everyone is on summer holidays.'

She sliced vegetables slowly, her eyes transfixed on her task as she picked up a carrot, examined it and gently cut it, as if creating a work of art. Kieran could not concentrate on his preparations, but glanced at her, taking in the shape of her eyes, the colour of her auburn hair, the pout of her lips. Her long hair fell over her blushed cheeks and black tight-fitting top. Her fingers were long and slender. Her demeanour was so confident, serene.

After a while, she stopped knife in hand and looked at him. 'Why are you staring at me?'

'Oh, pardon me, I'm not, it's just that, well I am writing an outline for a movie, and I've based a character on you.'

'On me? What do I do in the film?'

'Do? Nothing as yet, I mean I haven't got very far. It's still mostly an idea.'

'An idea? Well, what role to I play? You must know that at least.'

'You're the … love interest.'

'The female love interest, you mean? It takes two to tango, doesn't it.'

'Yes, yes of course. There is a man involved, it is a binary story, you know what I mean.'

'So who is the male love interest based on?'

'Ah, no one real, just a flawed character, an invention.'

'But my character can't be based on me. After all, you hardly know me.'

'True, I guess it was the impression that you gave me, the feeling I got that stuck with me when you first arrived. Somehow I was inspired and the mix of feeling, mood and emotion transformed into a character in my mind.'

'I'm surprised you have time for personal writing with your work on Zombies: The End Game.'

'It's called 'Vikings: Zombies Awake' actually. But they are intending for this film to be one of a series, if it's successful. Anyway, I'm not meant to be working on it full time while I'm here. This is supposed to be a getaway before we start production in September.'

'I'll be interested to hear how my character turns out. What's her name?'

'No name yet. But what about Helen?'

'Helen of Troy? The face that launched a thousand ships?'

'Yes, that's perfect. The movie does have an ocean theme.

They were silent for a while each concentrating on their cooking.

Kieran said, 'I would like to get to know you, I mean to help me with the characterisation.'

'All right, but we shall have to be careful. Your story will fall apart if the male lead turns out to be based on you.'

'No, no, it's not me at all. I promise to be just your friend. I'm not like Henry.'

'Do you mean you're not married, or not a chat-up artist?'

'Both, I mean neither. I'm not married.'

'Nor betrothed?

'No, not that either.'

'Ah, all right then, Sir Galahad. Let's be friends. Purely platonic relationship. That way I can relax while I'm here on me holliers and not worry about being chased by flattering, flirting men who have but one thing on their minds.'

6

Kieran awoke as usual and set to work preparing notes for the VFX supervisor. He needed to give him all the details of the scene of the zombies marching and attacking the castle so his team could prepare their work. The supervisor was a senior artist working from one of the major visual effects vendors in Soho. He had won an Emmy and been nominated for a BAFTA for previous films.

The VFX crew would be doing their own shoot in tandem with Kieran's cinematography team. They would cover the whole set with cameras. They needed to capture the position of everyone on set, actors and all of the camera crew, the lighting and textures of everything. They would recreate the entire set in three dimensions in software, and use it as a base to create computer graphic imagery to supplement or replace elements, including the main characters, and extend the set. Once the shots were complete, it was possible that little of Kieran's material would end up in the final released movie.

He could hardly concentrate on this detailed work. His mind in turmoil. What a fool I am. I let Henry beat me to her and he spoiled my chances. Now I've agreed to be her friend, he thought.

He had never won over a woman by pretending he wasn't interested in her. That was something only actors in movies could do. He couldn't play the aloof artist, heroin eyes, distanced gaze and hope that eventually she would throw herself at him, madly in love. No, he was going to have to win her over, but he had promised he wouldn't chase her. Unsure how to proceed, he finished his work and went down for a late breakfast.

'Good morning,' chirruped Kayley. 'What are you up to today? Working the whole time?'

'No, I just finished work on Zombie for the day. I could work on my story, or we could go on a drive if you like?'

'Let's go to the beach. I can read my book and we can enjoy the sunshine.'

Kieran drove them to Barleycove and they placed two big towels on the sand. Kayley took off her blouse and shorts to reveal her svelte figure and bikini for the first time.

The water was too cold for more than a quick dip, but Kieran acted playfully, splashing water at her. They ran back up the sand and crashed onto their towels.

Droplets of water slid down her back and shoulders as if caressing her skin. Kieran couldn't bear to look and turned and laid on his side. Soon Kayley propped herself up and opened her book. Kieran glanced over his shoulder. She was reading the screenplay of the Éric Rohmer film 'Love in the Afternoon'.

'Why are you reading that?' He asked.

'Josh gave it to me. He said if I wanted to be a filmmaker I had to read it as soon as possible.'

'How do you know Josh anyway?'

'He was a guest lecturer at my uni.'

'You had a thing with him?'

'We just became friendly.'

'Josh is married, you know?'

'I'm not going to break his home. It's just a casual relationship. He's an interesting man.'

Kieran sighed to himself in resignation. 'There are lots of interesting people in this business, but you should be careful.'

'I thought you and Josh were friends,' said Kayley

'We are friends, but our relationship is unequal in nature. He is rich and successful and I am, so far, a nobody.'

'Then why does he act like your friend?'

'Because I'm in the industry and I'm on the inside. But you learn not to take people too seriously. Everyone is friendly in the movie business. It's the nature of the business. There are talented people, egos, sensitivities. People are in show business to express themselves, and they seek affirmation. Everyone wants to be appreciated, loved. So everyone is friendly. But eventually the power dynamics of the relationships come to the fore.'

'So you think Josh will dump you someday?'

'If this movie goes well and I gain in stature, maybe not. Maybe we'll be more equal and our friendship will grow. I'm not suggesting he's disingenuous. It's the way of the world. Like the prince and the pauper. The prince will be whisked away one day, his attention demanded by others. The pauper, or showgirl, will be left behind and be just a pleasant memory to him.'

'So I shouldn't try and rise above my station?'

'Just be careful. I don't want you to get hurt.'

'Don't be silly. I can look after myself better than you think.'

'Perhaps you can, but people wonder why show business people have so many marriages and lovers. I think it's because, for them, it's all about the story. That's what they live and breathe, and why they're in the business in the first place. As kids they spent their time daydreaming. All kids daydream, but for people who become actors, singers, cameramen, directors, make-up artists, the story becomes who they are. They turn everything in their lives into a little scenario, a story. They can't help it.

'They meet someone and imagine a picture perfect life. They create a tableau in their minds and think yes, that's going to be great. Of course, the reality turns out differently, especially if two show folk get together. They each have a little scene that they are acting out – a double fantasy. In the end, it breaks apart because there was nothing holding it together in the first place – just a fantasy. Or they lose interest in the story and when someone else comes along they create a new one. They don't do it consciously. They just can't help themselves.

'So you have to be careful, giving yourself, your love. Your lover may be here today and off to another show tomorrow.'

'You are nice to worry about me. It's very sweet of you. It's like you're my best friend.'

Kieran's heart sank. He had heard the three worst words a girl could say to a boy, nice, sweet, friend. It was clear to him now that he had not created any sparks with Kayley. Her lips didn't tingle at the thought of his embrace. He became resigned to his status of a friendly chaperone.

After a while, Kayley glanced up from her book and said, 'Tell me about the story you're writing.'

'It's a love story, a bit like 'Gone with the Wind'.'

'Oh, a big costume drama epic set in wartime.'

'No, no, just the tension between the two main characters. They are destined for one another but circumstances prevent them from staying together.'

'Or is it more like Casablanca? They meet, fall in love but are torn apart.'

'Now that's a good idea, I like that. But maybe more like 'Titanic'. The lovers were from different backgrounds, so they were forbidden to be together. But they fell in love anyway.'

'In the end they are separated in a big dramatic scene when the ship sinks?'

'Actually, at the end of my story they sail away, leaving the world they knew behind to be together.'

'Like 'The Graduate'?'

'Yeah, that's a good ending.'

''The Graduate' was a romantic comedy. At least that was the genre the film critics squeezed it into. Is that what your story is?'

'Not really. I don't think I can do comedy. It's more of a coming of age romance perhaps.'

'Ah, so they're teenagers like, 'Romeo and Juliet.'

'I'm not sure, but I do have an atmosphere and a look in my mind.'

'Where are you up to? Do you have an ending?'

'I'm working on creating the tension between the two main characters. There has to be a challenge to overcome. She can't just fall into his arms.'

'Maybe when they first meet he's dismissive of her. After all, they are from different backgrounds, so the boy doesn't notice the girl at first,' suggested Kayley.

'Maybe the tension comes because they are at different stages in life.'

'Oh, like you and me?'

'You're right. It is as if we are on different rungs of the same ladder. I didn't want to push you away when we first met. I was wrapped up in my own journey. But I felt attracted to you.'

'I thought you decided I wasn't worth the effort. You were right, of course. I'm too young for you, inexperienced. Just a silly graduate looking for a start. You're a successful cinematographer, now to be a director.'

'But I liked you right away. I thought you were beautiful and intriguing. I don't think we are that different and our age doesn't matter. I'm not that much older than you.'

'But we're just friends Kieran. I like you, I do. Maybe I can help you. We can work on the story together.'

'No, Kayley, this is a personal endeavour. What is your ambition in film making anyway? Do you want to write, produce?'

'I see myself directing. But maybe the best way into the industry is through producing. There seem to be a lot of female producers. Maybe I can get a junior role somewhere.'

'Where are you from, you sound like you're from Cork.'

'I'm from Dublin, but my parents moved to Cork so they could afford a better place. They commute to Dublin or London when they get work. My father is a musician.'

'Playing in a band?'

'Yes, lots of bands. But for money, he works as a session musician, mostly for TV and commercials. He's worked on film soundtracks as well.'

'What about your mother?'

'She's a painter. But for money, she's a production designer and does bits and bobs on film sets. They both take whatever work they can get.'

'So your family are in the industry. Well, there you are. So that's why you studied film.'

'I guess so. My parents sent me to music and dance lessons. Early on I took up acting and I did two years at a drama school in England before uni. But I'm more interested in the whole creative process, how movies are put together.'

He was astonished at his naivety. He had been giving her advice about show folk and she was from a show family. He felt foolish, but his fascination with her grew with every word she said. She wasn't just vivacious and attractive. She was intelligent, driven and talented.

'So what will you do with your story? Will you write a synopsis and treatment and tout it around to see if you can get development funding?'

'You're one step ahead of me all the way, Kayley. I'm down here to work on Zombie. My story is just an idea that came into my mind. But you're right. If it's going to get anywhere I'd better get serious and map out its trajectory.'

Kieran and Kayley were inseparable from then on. For the next few days, they ate breakfast, lunch and dinner together and read by the fire at night. They went for walks across the hills and swam at Barleycove.

After Henry had tried to seduce her, Kieran felt he had to rise to the challenge and was determined to have her. But now, he felt a pang in his heart as he thought of her. Whenever he glanced up and saw her face a thrill of excitement tingled through him and his pulse jumped. She is a vision he thought, but so much more. She is a talent, a bright, beautiful personality. Now he wanted her love, not for her to simply to fall for his charms.

Kieran played the role of a perfect gentleman, turning his back when Kayley took off her bikini and put on her clothes for the drive back up to Inisheen from the beach. Actually, he did have a few quick glances at her teardrop breasts.

At night they kissed on each cheek French style and went to their separate rooms.

'Good night Kieran,' Kayley called from her bed.

'Good night Kayley,' Kieran called back.

7

The next morning there was just one email from Zak
It read, 'Kieran, some more of the crew have arrived from LA. Come over to my house this afternoon, I want you to meet the production designer and the VFX producer will be here as well. A casual get to know each other. We'll have a drink on the lawn.'

At breakfast he said, 'Kayley, I have to go out this afternoon.'

'Oh, can I come?'

'Zak invited, I mean commanded, me to go over to see him at his house near Bantry.'

'So it's work.'

'I guess so. He said we would have a drink on the lawn.'

'Go on, bring me along. You can have a drink and I'll drive us home,' said Kayley.

It seemed a good idea to have a non-drinking driver. But he wondered about Kayley's motives. 'I think Zak might be gay you know, Kayley.'

'Don't be silly. I'm not interested in Zak, although I've never met him. But I would like to see the big house and meet some industry people,' she said.

Kieran had no idea at all if Zak was gay. He had met him several times as well as seen him on a few video calls. He had big arm muscles and clearly worked out, unlike Kieran. He had a few tattoos and piercings. He seemed neat and tasteful, but that didn't mean he was gay.

In the late afternoon they set out for Bantry in Kieran's car. The drive took a little over half an hour. They drove past the statue of St Brendan on the town square by the harbour as Kieran followed the purple line on his satnav along the coast road.

Just outside Bantry they noticed a sign, 'Kilnaruane Pillar Stone'.

Kayley said, 'Please let's stop and have a look.'

They pulled over and walked up a muddy path into a field. In the middle of the field was a cordoned off area and a stone pillar about two metres tall. They went up close and walked around it, examining its carved surface. There was a carving of a boat, a currach, being rowed by four oarsmen and a helmsman. They were surrounded by crosses as if floating in the sea.

'It looks like Saint Brendan. What a great story that is. I'd like to make that movie. A group of monks led by a visionary, sail off across uncharted oceans in search of paradise, but find America instead,' said Kieran.

They returned to the car and continued on the road. 'There it is,' said Kayley pointing to a big Georgian house at the top of a long driveway surrounded by large ornamental gardens. Kieran stopped at the imposing iron entry gates.

'Maybe he's staying in the cottage out the back,' Kayley laughed.

'I think not. I have to ring the bell.'

He pushed the buzzer and after a few moments the gates swung open and they continued up the driveway. He stopped the car in front of the large stoop that led to a portico and double front doors.

Before they could get out of the car a man in a tweed jacket emerged from a side door and waved at Kieran urging him to drive the car over to him and said, 'You can't park there, for heaven's sake, not in that.'

He directed them to a side parking area with a sign that read - Tradesman's Entrance. 'I should have rented a Merc for this,' Kieran mumbled.

The man ushered them in at the tradesman's door and through the kitchen into the entrance hall of the house. 'Wait here,' he said. They stood and admired the handsome double semi-circular staircase that wound its way up three floors. Above, inside a dome painted powder blue, light gleamed in through stained glass windows.

'Impressive, Kieran, but we don't even warrant the front door,' Kayley teased him with a big grin on her face.

Soon a maid came and waving her hand as if they were naughty children shooed them out to the back of the house through a magnificent double living area with two huge fireplaces, multiple leather sofas, tall oak bookcases filled with expensive leather-bound volumes and major artworks on the walls. She lead them out through floor-to-ceiling glass doors onto a large, wide, immaculate lawn tastefully decorated with ornamental shrubs and formal flower beds. It overlooked Bantry Bay with a magnificent view of the mountains of the Beara Penninsula across the bay.

Set off to one side was a white wrought iron table and eight chairs where several people were lounging. Zak stood up and walked over to greet them.

'Kieran, so glad to have you here,' he said. He smiled at Kayley looking her up and down.

'Zak, may I present my friend Kayley. She is staying with me. I hope you don't mind.'

'Very pleased to meet you, Kayley,' he said, ignoring Kieran. Smiling he bent his arm for her to hold and arm in arm they walked towards the table with Kieran following.

Nope, he doesn't seem gay to me. Not at all, he thought cursing his bad decision making once again.

'Hey Kieran,' said Melanie, the VFX producer from Soho.

'Melanie!, muah, muah.' They kissed each other on the cheek.

'This is Lukasz, the production designer. I don't think you've met as yet.'

'Hi Lukasz, no, we haven't met. I don't think you were around when I was in LA,' said Kieran.

'Yesh, Kiera-a-a-n, zhach is correct, I was in Budapest working on *Barbarians: The Coming*,' intoned Lukasz in a thick Polish accent.

Zak and Kayley continued to the end of the garden admiring the view and chatting. Kieran sat down and a waitress brought him an electric blue drink in a wide glass.

'Here you are, sir, a Cobalt Daquiri,' she said. Kieran grimaced and she said. 'Can I get you something else?'

'Champagne, please,' said Kieran his eyes fixed on Zak and Kayley.

He chatted with Lukasz and Melanie and guzzled champagne. The waitress was very attentive and his glass never seemed to be more than half empty. After what seemed a long time, Zak and Kayley came over to the table and joined them. As the sun went down behind the distant clouds in the southwest the sky radiated gold, then pink and finally a tequila sunrise red as the Beara Peninsula fell into darkness.

Kieran became engaged in a long conversation, almost impossible to understand, with Lukasz. The champagne made him animated, he waved his arms in explanation and nodded his head vigorously in agreement with whatever Lukasz said.

As darkness finally took hold, Zak stood up. 'Well everyone, thank you for a very enjoyable mixer this evening. We have work to do tomorrow so I think we should all get going.'

The soiree was over and Zak ushered Kieran and Kayley into the house. Kieran was fearful he might shove them out the tradesman's entrance and was relieved when he walked them to the front door, which the maid opened for them.

As they were leaving he said, 'I'm having a party here tomorrow night. More of the crew will be coming down from Dublin so you must come, and please be sure to bring Kayley,' he said smiling at her. 'There are plenty of rooms here for you both to stay, so no need to worry about driving home after drinking. See you tomorrow.'

Kieran slumped in the passenger seat as Kayley drove them back to Inisheen. 'You and Zak certainly got on well,' he said.

'Yes, he is a very interesting man,' said Kayley.

She drove with confidence. Kieran kept looking at the side of her face, her features were so clear, streaking from shadow to dark as lights of cars and houses flashed by.

As they climbed the stairs to their rooms he put his arm around her waist and she turned to him. Her eyes stared into his and her lips pouted. They kissed and embraced. He said, 'I can't help myself, I've fallen for you.'

'You're very nice, Kieran. I like you a lot, too much maybe,' she said.

They kissed again, but she soon pulled away. 'You should get some sleep Kieran, get the champagne out of your system. Good night.'

She disappeared into her room leaving Kieran's emotions and body tangled in his desire for her.

While Kieran was checking his email the next morning he regretted kissing Kayley. He felt he had let his guard down, given away his feelings too stridently. But she hadn't pushed him away. She had kissed him back. Was he reading the signs correctly he wondered?

He went downstairs and Kayley was making breakfast wearing a t-shirt and bare legs. After breakfast he said, 'I'm sorry about last night Kayley. The champagne did get to me I suppose, but in vino veritas.'

'Don't worry, Kieran, your attention is flattering. I can't help liking it. You've been good company for the last few days. I've enjoyed our time together.'

Could it be that she was falling for him he wondered? Maybe she wasn't in love with him, but falling for his charm would be fine with him after all.

He put his hand gently in hers and she squeezed his fingers. 'I feel like you've been courting me like a real gentleman.' she said.

'Not going too fast for you I hope?'

'No, not too fast.'

He moved closer to her and went to kiss her but she moved her face away.

'I'm still not ready, Kieran, but I feel something for you now.'

'You're a mysterious woman, Kayley. You seemed so passionate with those other guys. I think we can risk some intimacy.'

'Not now, not today. It's different with people of my own age, from the same year at uni. Somehow it's natural, casual. With you, it seems more serious. I need to take my time. But we have time, don't we? Let's see how we feel after the party tonight. I'm looking forward to that.'

Kieran determined to play his part and stay the gentleman. He was nice and entertaining for the rest of the day. They played badminton in the garden and lazed on deck chairs. The afternoon wore on and the time came to go to the party.

They each packed an overnight bag and Kieran drove, this time he knew where to park. They walked around the house to the front steps and went in through the main door. From the entrance hall, Kieran could see a drinks table in the living room and made straight for it. He picked up two glasses of champagne and turned around to find Kayley. She was still at the front door and waved for him to come over.

'Come on, we have to be shown our rooms first,' she said. The maid took them upstairs and showed them two adjoining bedrooms. 'I'll get the bags from the car, you don't need to worry, I'll meet you inside' said Kayley.

Kieran wandered through the living rooms and out into the garden still with a glass in each hand. The first one was now empty and he set it down. There were already a few dozen people talking, drinking and eating canapés.

'Hi Kieran, come and meet my team,' said a big man with a full beard. It was Jordan the Director of Photography. He was standing with several guys dress in plaid shirts and big shoes. One of them slapped him on the back and said, 'I'm so looking forward to working with you, I love your work.'

Several glasses of champagne later there was a brief moment of silence. Jordan leaned over to him and said softly, 'I'm sorry. In my opinion it's unfair. I just wanted you to know.'

'Unfair? What are you talking about Jordan?'

'Bringing in Lars. I think it's unnecessary, and not fair to you.'

'Lars? You don't mean Lars Halkonen, do you? Nobody mentioned him to me.'

'You haven't heard? Well maybe it's just a rumour then. I'm relieved, like I said, I'm against it. So I'm glad I was wrong.'

'Where did you hear that Jordan?'

'Actually Kieran, I don't remember. Rumours, that's all. You hear all kinds of bullshit in this business. I'm looking forward to working with you. Cheers.'

They clinked glasses and Kieran gulped his champagne. 'Hey Jordan, I'm going to walk around a bit, see you later.'

He felt unnerved and confused. He was dizzy, his heart racing and hot flushes pulsed through his face. I knew it, I knew I couldn't trust that bastard Zak.

Lars Halkonen had been Assistant Director on 'Barbarians: The Coming'. So Lukasz and Melanie must have known. Everyone knows but me. That must be why he invited me over for drinks last night. He was going to tell me then, but the rat started hitting on Kayley instead. Damn coward. At least he didn't fire me by email or text.

He picked up another glass of champagne and went out to the lawn. He hadn't seen Kayley since she went to the car and he wandered around looking for her.

The party was in full swing and a band set up on the lawn and started playing. The singer belted out in a Cork accent, 'Brown Sugar, how come you taste so good, ooh, yea.' The crowd cheered and dancers swept onto the lawn swirling to the old beat. Actually, they are quite good dancers, thought Kieran. That's what you get with show folk, they aren't shy and they're talented.

With drink in hand Kieran wandered all over the house looking for Kayley, and Zak, but caught sight of neither of them.

In a corridor on the second floor, he bumped into one of the line producers. 'Hi Kieran, I'm sorry to hear the news man,' he said and continued on down the corridor patting Kieran on the back as he went. That's the second time tonight someone's patted me on the back. Now he felt rage building up inside of him.

Angry, he wandered through the house. On the top floor, he heard voices in a room with its door ajar. He heard Kayley laugh. He pushed the door open and to see Zak and a small group of people including Kayley, sitting on sofas around a glass coffee table. It looked as if, yes, they were doing lines. As he approached someone tossed a magazine onto the table covering up whatever was going on.

Kayley looked at him, her eyes bright, a big smile on her face. Zak said, 'Hey Kieran, how are you doing? You look a bit wiped out sport. Maybe you need a break.'

'Zak, I need to talk to you,' said Kieran.

'Sure, let's take breakfast together in the morning,'

'I mean right now Zak, now, I have to talk to you,' said Kieran, his eyes glaring.

Zak seemed to get the message, nodded and stood up. 'Let's go out on the balcony, I have a few minutes.'

They walked through a pair of French doors onto a balcony that looked down on the front garden and driveway, facing away from the raging party at the back of the mansion. The sounds of the band playing 'Knights in White Satin' reverberated around the gardens.

'What's on your mind, Kieran?'

'Zak, are the rumours true?'

'The rumours are always true.'

'So you're replacing me with Lars Halkonen?'

'No, not replacing you. I'm just bringing him onboard.'

'Why?'

'Because he's a comer. You're a comer, don't worry.'

'I'm not working for Lars, no way.'

'No, you're not. You work for me.'

'Then why bring him in? Three's a crowd.'

'He's available, that's why. I think he'll bring something to the show, add a new dimension to what we're doing. Besides, it'll keep the producers quiet. You're an unknown quantity and he has a track record. The money is a very important part of the process, as you are aware.'

'What's he going to do? What will I be left with?'

'We still have to figure that out, but we have time. I've been pleased with the progress we've made together here. We've gotten through it all much quicker than I expected. We can work through everything. Just stay cool, got it? I gotta go back into my guests now.'

'Your guests? I came here with Kayley.'

'Yes, but you two aren't together are you? I mean you're not an item. She's sharing Josh's house with you, right?'

'What's your interest in her Zak?'

'No interest, or lots of interest. It's not your place to ask. She's a talented girl, I like her.'

'That's right Zak, she's a girl.'

'I mean woman, she's not a teenager. She is an adult and she can look after herself. Besides, Josh and I are friends. I told him I'd look after her. She'll be fine. But you? Frankly, you look a mess. You ought to go sleep it off. As I said, let's do breakfast, all right?'

Kieran turned around and went back into the room. Kayley was in earnest conversation with a guy with a topknot. 'Kayley, come on let's go,' he said slowly.

'Go? Kieran, you go. You look like you need a lie-down. I'm fine, I'll catch up with you later or in the morning.' She returned to her conversation.

Kieran felt helpless and marched out of the room and down the stairs. He picked up an unopened bottle of champagne and continued out the front door and into his car.

He drove through the town of Bantry as carefully as he could. There was a Garda patrol stopped on the high street. The two Gardaí looked at him as he drove past but they didn't move.

He arrived home and opened the champagne. He awoke in the middle of the night, his head in his arms on his table, and stumbled onto his bed.

8

Twillip- twillip twillip-twillip. He was still in his clothes and he fished his phone out of his pocket. 'Yeragh, hello ... Kayley, where are you? ... Oh at the house where I left you of course ... No, I didn't abandon you ... Well I'm sorry if you feel abandoned. You seemed to be having a good time ... Alright alright, I'll come and get you as soon as possible. See you in forty-five minutes or so ... You were worried about me? ... That's wonderful to hear, but I'm grand thanks be. See you soon.'

Kieran had a quick shower and put on clean clothes. He was about to leave but changed his mind and took his shirt off. I should have a shave. After my performance last night I'd better be on my best form, he thought.

Clean and sooth he drove down the road to Bantry once more. He felt pleasantly surprised that Kayley had said she was worried about him. She genuinely seemed to care about him. He drove into the side car park again. The side door of the house was open so he went in that way. 'Morning all,' he beamed at the staff as he paraded through the kitchen and into the entrance hall.

He saw a group of people on the back lawn having brunch, and spotted Zak. He texted Kayley and she came downstairs with her bag over her shoulder, carrying Kieran's overnight bag in her arms.

'All recovered from last night?' she asked.

'I'm fine. Let's get of here, but first I need to see Zak. Wait in the car for me, I'll only be a minute,' said Kieran.

He put on a big smile and walked nonchalantly into the garden. Zak was serving himself what looked like kedgeree from a silver bain-maire.

'Kieran, you're looking surprisingly dapper and well this morning,' said Zak.

'I was a bit under the weather yesterday. I had terrible hay fever, I was sneezing and weeping all day. But today I'm fine. That's the summer weather for you. It was a great party last night. Ah it was, and thanks for your hospitality. Next time don't have so much champagne perhaps. Go on, it was a grand evening.'

'That's nice, thank you, Kieran. You seemed a bit upset last night, but you seem very cool now.'

'Zak, me upset? No no, it was the terrible hay fever that was afflicting me so. Today I have perfectly clear vision. I can see all the way to Kerry. Actually I can see all the way to Kerry from here. Fantastic place you found. I should have mentioned that earlier.'

'Yea, it's wonderful, isn't it? Last year I was in Romania, but Ireland is so much more interesting. You know, I love your country. The people are so friendly.'

'Friendly and talented Zak, don't forget that. Also, us locals, we know the lie of the land, you know. We know where the best locations are, the time of day, inside knowledge. That can never be underestimated.'

'Of course not, we value what the local crew can bring to the project. I'm counting on you Kieran, I need you.'

'Do you also need Lars Halkonen?'

'Yes, I do, as I explained. He'll keep the heat off my back. But don't worry so much Kieran. You're the main guy, my point man. Don't screw up a good thing.'

'I won't Zak. You can rely on me, that's for sure. I'm here for you night and day. I'll deliver your vision for you. You have my word.'

'Kieran, I knew about you. I had an instinct, a hunch. You know how to play the scene, the way to go. By the way, you have taste as well. I mean Kayley, she's special. You have an eye for talent.'

'You like her, do you?'

'Yes I do. You make sure she's on set. Give her a role of some kind.'

'Zak, I've no problem with that or anything. As you said, we'll work through it all.'

'Let's take a few days off. I'll talk to you later in the week.'

Kieran's hands were on fire as he marched away from Zak through the house and out the big front door, down the stoop and around to the tradesman's car park. He hadn't even been aware that Josh knew Zak.

But of course, Josh knows everybody, he thought. He felt as if he had been set up by the three of them, Josh, Kayley and Zak.

Kieran felt energised by his talk with Zak, emboldened. No longer did he feel obliged to be polite, nice. He determined to take control.

In the car park, Kayley was leaning on the car staring at her phone. Without hesitation he demanded, 'Did you sleep with him?'

'None of your business, but no, of course not. Who do you think I am? I don't go to bed with just anyone. You guys have inflated ideas of yourselves. You have no morals. You judge women by your own low standards.'

'How can I believe you? You were coked up or worse.'

'I was not, I didn't do any drugs at all.'

'I saw, on the table, you were all doing lines of something.'

'You didn't see that at all. You were so drunk, how do you know what you saw? Talk about the pot calling the kettle black.'

'What about Josh? You had a thing with him too, didn't you? Did he tell you that Zak was going to be down here? Was this all a set-up with me as the mug?'

'No, I did not sleep with Josh. Yes, Josh mentioned that Zak would be down here. He told me that you would be here as well. He said that it wouldn't do any harm to be on holiday with some people in the industry. That if I were serious about my career, I should involve myself in the movie business and that it would be a waste of time to fritter my summer away in Greece drinking and dancing.

'I didn't deceive anyone. I didn't ask any favours or make any promises. I'm just being myself and trying my best.'

'Are you telling me the truth? It's just that I care about you, for you. I only want to be with you.'

'Am I telling the truth? What about you, Kieran? Don't you have something to tell me? You said you weren't married.'

'I'm not.'

'Oh, well Henry told me ...'

'He told you about Cheryl?'

'Yes, you're engaged. So you don't only want to be with me, do you?'

'It's over between us, me and Cheryl. Why do you think I'm here all alone? I didn't want to burden you or Henry with my troubles. The truth is, I'm glad she broke it off. I was sad, but then I met you and I knew, for the first time, I really knew who I wanted. It's you Kayley, you're the one that I want. At least we can give it a try, can't we? I know now that you're attracted to me.'

'I am I suppose. But when I think of you cheating on your fiance and telling me who I can sleep with!'

'I should have told you earlier, I'm sorry. But I didn't want to be talking about another woman. I wanted to talk about you. I fell for you, head over heels. I came down here to be alone. You can ask Henry. He'll tell you that's what I told him when he showed up weeks early. I wasn't looking for another lover. I wanted peace, solitude. Then you arrived. I think it was meant to be, you and me.'

'So you've really split up with Cheryl?'

'It was a long time in the making. We haven't been lovers for ages. She was always working, making excuses. I've been alone for what seemed an eternity of wasted time, until I met you.'

He put his arms around her. She gently put one arm, then another around his shoulders. She buried her face in his chest. He combed his fingers through her long hair as if to soothe her. She looked up at him and they kissed.

'We must make love, otherwise, we'll never know if we were right for each other.'

'All right, Kieran. Let's go home.'

He drove once more down the road to Inisheen and at a fork in the road they were stopped by a herd of cows coming towards them. A car approached from the other fork with two young men inside. The driver was Michael, the boy that Kayley had been with at the house the previous week.

'Hey Kayley!' he shouted as he pulled his car up on the side of the road.

She opened the car door and went over to talk to them. She had her overnight bag over her shoulder just as she did when she got in the car. He couldn't tell whether it was by accident or design.

Kieran could half hear what they were saying over the mooing of the cows and the clip-clopping of their hooves along the road towards him.

'... we're going to Clonakilty, it's going to be a big night, come with us.'

'I'd love to but I can't. I'm with him.'

'Come with us. It's going to be a big party.'

'But I said I'd go with him.'

'Drop him. What do you want that old guy for?'

She continued talking to the boys, leaning in the window of the car. By now there was a queue of cars behind Kieran, eager to get going again. One of them leaned on the horn, drowning out what Kayley was saying.

The herd of cows reached a low point in the fence just ahead of his car and without hesitation, one by one they jumped over and into the field. At the back of the herd, the farmer kept them moving with a stick that he trailed on the ground behind them. Soon the last cow jumped into the field and the farmer tipped his hat to Kieran.

Kieran started the engine and felt his foot press on the accelerator. Soon he reached a bend in the road and he glanced in his rear view mirror to see Kayley still talking, oblivious that Kieran had gone. As he rounded the bend she fell out of view. He didn't know why he left her but he felt she would be fine with her friends. He had no plan, so he concentrated on the road ahead.

Soon he was pulling into the driveway of Inisheen. He went to his computer and searched various websites. Ah, perfect, he thought. A few clicks, then ping, the confirmation was in his email inbox. Another ping and he had received the boarding pass on his phone.

I should just about make it, he thought. He quickly packed up his things and threw his bag and computer into the car. He drove as fast as he dared, remembering how slowly he had driven through West Cork on his way down from Dublin. Now he hurried to get out. He didn't want to be late.

Just under two hours later, he left his car in the long-term car park at Cork Airport and found the departure lounge. He looked at the list of arrivals and departures. There is it, Aer Lingus, Cork to London Heathrow.

As he waited at the gate he read through his story. He had now figured out most of the plot points and many of the beats, but had yet to come up with a satisfactory ending. He had moved on from the misty boat scene at Crookhaven. He put various scenarios to test in his mind, rejecting each one in turn. He picks her up in his arms and carries her off into the night with flashes of light and smoke. No, no good. He gets down on one knee and proposes marriage. No, damn it.

What he did feel sure about was that the guy gets the girl and they set off into an unknown future full of love and hope. I guess I'll figure it out in London, he thought, and slapped his laptop shut.

His mind drifted back momentarily to Kayley and his time with her. It already seemed like a movie that he had seen last week. He knew it was a good movie but he struggled to remember the exact details.

He looked at the date on his smartwatch. It was two weeks and six days since he had walked with Cheryl on Killiney Strand.

****

No.2

The Curator

1

Louis awoke to the sound of his young baby crying as Sandrine walked through the open bedroom door from the bathroom to the baby's cot. 'Petite Julie, calme-toi.'

She picked up the baby in her arms and gently rocked her back and forth. Sitting on the end of the bed she opened her white blouse and put the baby to her breast. The composition and the haunting beauty of Sandrine reminded him of the Picasso painting, *Maternity,* from 1909.

Louis sat up in bed and admired the beautiful scene. As in the painting, Sandrine was so absorbed in feeding her child that the rest of the world seemed not to exist for her. Like a statue come to life, her small tender movements and serene smile evoked the universal image of motherhood.

How lucky he was, he thought. Sandrine looks so happy. She was, at that very moment, the image of perfection. The room was warm and filled with the soft clinging smell of new birth. The only sound was the whispered sucking of the baby on Sandrine's full breast.

Sandrine was actually not that young a mother. Louis remembered the night they had met, nearly twelve years earlier. He smiled to himself; she looks even more beautiful now than she did then. She was ten years younger than Louis. They met in Paris and were married two years later, but baby Julie had been her first pregnancy. How time flies, he thought. What happened to those years? Still, no matter, here we are, a proper family at last.'

Sandrine looked up at Louis and laughed softly, 'You had better make your own breakfast, cheri.'

He padded downstairs in his socks and made toast and porridge. Soon Sandrine came into the kitchen and said, 'The baby is asleep now.'

Louis watched her as she picked up his empty plates from the table, turned and took them to the sink. She was self-assured, her eyes bright and loving. He admired her hands and her behind as she turned her back. He felt a stirring and remembered the feeling of pressing his fingers around her curves.

He loved her, but why her? Of all the women he had met before Sandrine, of all the women he encountered day by, why was it she, in particular, that had taken his love? What was her unique beauty that captured him? He seemed to have forgotten. All he could perceive was feminine, maternal beauty, not Sandrine's uniqueness.

'I'm off now my love,' he said rising from his chair.

Louis took the Tube to work. He liked to read on the train and enjoyed the distraction of being embroiled in a story. But more importantly he sought the anonymity that hiding behind a book cover gave him. No one in the carriage paid the least attention to him while they assumed he was reading. He could observe people unnoticed. A woman somewhere in the carriage would always grab his attention. This morning it was a young dark haired woman opposite him. She looked at her phone, absorbed. Now bored, with no new messages, she put her phone in her handbag and gazed up at the ceiling, lost in some other world.

Louis peered out over the top of his book, trying to decide about her. He was no longer so quick to classify the women he saw as ones that he would like to be with or not. He took his time to consider whether they possessed the indefinable quality, that something that a woman had to have to attract him. His blood was not so quick to rush and fill him with desire as it used to be. Married, aging, he was just a passive observer.

The beauty of women and the allure of sex filled his mind. The intoxicating mixture of anticipation and uncertainty tore at his heart. I'm just same as everyone else in that regard, he thought. But it was a woman's face, expression and gestures that interested him. He imagined that in these stolen moments he witnessed their intimate inner thoughts. That the mystery of their essence was being revealed to him, conveyed through subtle movements, a smile or frown, the smallest things.

The dark haired woman stood up and moved towards the doors. The train came to a sliding stop at Victoria and she disappeared into the crowd. What if I had met this woman before Sandrine? Would I have fallen in love with her, wanted to have a child with her? The constant yet fleeting presence of women I will never see again. Is it enough that I feel their charm without giving in to it? I feel life passing me by, frustrated not to have held each one of these women even for an instant.

The train arrived at Charring Cross and the doors of the carriage burst open with a hiss. With the madding crowd, he trundled out the doors, up the stairs, along the never-ending corridor and past the buskers. He felt like a fish in a giant school, turning with all the others, gaping, swimming to and fro. Being in a crowded street or train was a tonic for him. It brought him peace and his best ideas came to him while he flowed through the stream of people. Eventually, he made his way out into the street and walked across Trafalgar Square to the National Gallery where he worked.

Louis was a curator and enjoyed his role. He had joined the Gallery before he met Sandrine and had made his way up the echelons, gaining his Masters Degree and publishing various treatises along the way. Now he was in a senior position and his career was set. One day he may even be appointed Head of Curation. His life was solid, stable, built on sound foundations, and he thought it would stay that way.

He nodded good morning to the gallery staff as he made his way up to his office. He walked with a slight swagger, his left hand in his suit jacket pocket. He affected a reserved, but friendly demeanour. He had been brought up to understand the importance of projecting an appropriate air.

The lift door opened on his level and he said good morning to lovely Emily, the receptionist. She was definitely to his taste and had that certain something. But he was sure not to let his impure thoughts be noticed by anyone. No, he just admired the beauty of women. That was all. After all, I do work in the arts, he assured himself.

Although he sometimes imagined how it would be to embrace and kiss the women he observed, he had not had an affair with anyone since he moved in with Sandrine, one year after they had first met. He would remain faithful, of course, until ... until the baby grows up at least. I have that responsibility now. I can't let my family down. Then I'll be an old man in any case.

Louis met Sandrine on a working visit to Paris where she was employed at the Musée d'Orsay. A year later she moved from Paris to London. The next year they married and bought their apartment at Bayswater. Although he was brought up in London, Louis' mother was from Paris and he had spent much time there. He had attended the Lycée Français in London and spoke fluent French. Indeed, being bi-lingual had been a great boost to his career.

That day he had a lunch appointment with an old friend called David. One o'clock arrived and he made his way to the National Dining Rooms in the Sainsbury Wing. The lift doors swished open and he went out into the never-ending stream of people.

There were thousands of people of all shapes, sizes and nationalities jabbering in a multitude of languages. Like a lion looking at a herd of zebra, he watched them meld together in a jumble of colour and shapes, until his eyes picked out an individual, a woman gazing at a painting lost in thought, or reading on a bench.

He breezed along the corridor to the restaurant, nodding to the staff along the way. David was waiting for him sitting at a table by a window looking out onto Trafalgar Square. 'Louis, how are the baby and Sandrine?'

'They are both very well. Sandrine is in a state of bliss, and the baby sleeps most of the time.'

David had attended the same university as Louis, although he was a bit older. After a while their conversation slowed and they both sat in silence.

David noticed Louis' head turning from left to right as he watched passers by in the street below. 'Stop undressing the girls as they walk by Louis,' he said.

'I'm not, I'm only looking, looking at their eyes, and their faces.'

'Why are you looking at all Louis? You have a beautiful wife at home.'

'A cat can look at a queen they say. Nothing wrong with looking, you know that's all I ever do,' said Louis.

'You're doing a bit more than looking in your mind. It's still a sin,' David laughed.

'Really? You think it wrong of me? I am a red blooded man. I can't help it if there are beautiful women around. What am I supposed to do, close my eyes?'

'Avert your eyes Louis. Avert your eyes and don't be so obvious.'

'Am I that obvious? Maybe it's just because you know me. I never see a woman look back at me, never.'

'Ah, maybe they're averting their eyes. Perhaps they are more polite than you.'

'Women are never attracted to me. In all these years I have never had an affair, unlike you David. If there is one thing I am incapable of now, it's flirting with a girl. I have no idea what to say and no reason to speak to her,' said Louis.

'Yes, well, at least I'm honest with myself. I like women and sometimes they are attracted to me. I don't pretend to be disinterested like you do. Then sometimes, you know, one thing leads to another. A glance, chemistry, the brush of hands, that's how men and women get together. It just happens.'

'You're as married as I am, David. Besides, what do you mean, I'm disinterested?'

'I've seen it many times over the years. You eye up a girl, she looks back at you and you turn away. I've seen several girls become attracted to you, even approach you. But you always act is if you don't like them and brush them away.'

'Have I done that? I can't believe it. Who was attracted to me?'

'Lucinda is one example. Remember her a couple of years ago? You really missed out there. She's married now. But you only want to look, not actually make love. Isn't that right?'

'It's true I sometimes feel that marriage closes me in and I want to escape. I miss the time when I could experience the pang of anticipation. But I avoid situations where I might get entangled with other women. I rarely go to parties. I don't go to clubs looking for women and I don't chase women full stop. That doesn't mean I don't desire something more. But you do all those things. You go out with your colleagues to clubs, leave your wife at home and look for girls. Of course, sometimes you find one.'

'Louis, I'm mostly faithful to my wife although I may deceive her now and then, but you're wrong. I don't go hunting for women. I go out for entertainment, a good time with my friends. I don't look for it, but I don't refuse it either. I let nature take its course. The women I've known are real people, flesh and blood. Life isn't planned, laid out like a perfect composition. Occasionally something happens and I meet someone. It seems to me that your way is detached, cold. You pretend you're faithful, but cheat in your mind ten times a day.'

Louis had no answer to David's disturbing observations. He stared once again out into the square with nothing to say. Am I really so transparent, such a hypocrite? he wondered.

David interrupted Louis' soul searching, 'Cheer up old boy. Don't take me so seriously. I was only ribbing you. Speaking of parties, you know it's my 50th birthday in June don't you?'

'Yes, of course, I remember. How are you going to celebrate it?'

'We'll go to the country house for the weekend. I'm inviting a bunch of friends, old and new, for a house party. You must come, bring the family.'

'In June the baby will only be four months old. I don't think we'll be able to make it.'

'I know, but I can't move the date of my birthday. You're invited, remember that. Come by yourself. Maybe by then you and Sandrine will be ready for a break. Having a new baby puts a lot of pressure on couples, believe me. It might be healthy for you to leave them alone for a day or two. Keep it in mind anyway.'

2

L ouis soon forgot his conversation with David. Family life took over and the weeks sped by. David had been right about the pressure on him and Sandrine. The baby no longer slept through the night and he was tired and ragged. Sandrine encouraged him to go. 'Cheri it's just for the weekend and don't worry about us. You need a break. Besides, David is your oldest friend and it's his 50th.'

On Saturday afternoon he drove down the A40 to the house at Chalfont St Giles.

Sandrine kissed him, 'Au revoir cheri, see you Monday.'

He felt light hearted as he drove. He had no expectations for the weekend, save to get a little bit drunk and have a good time. He remembered his conversation with David and thought he had been unfair. He had been faithful to Sandrine, not just in body. Being married suited him. He was happier not having to worry about relationships with women. He could pursue his interests without the pressure of having to find a girlfriend.

When he first met Sandrine they were attracted to each other straight away. He asked her out to dinner. Perhaps it was just that he was an Englishman who could actually speak French, but she enjoyed his company. She smiled and looked at him amorously, held his hand and moved closer to him. Her big green eyes stared into his.

Louis returned to London after a short while, but they kept up their relationship, long distance. He regularly went to Paris for weekends, and Sandrine came to London often as well. It was not exactly a hardship for either of them as Louis loved Paris and Sandrine London.

Sandrine worked in administration but was ambitious and determined to pursue a career in arts centre management. Louis knew many people in the arts scene in London, and was quite socially active in those days.

It soon became apparent that having Sandrine at his side at dinner parties and functions was advantageous. It seemed to transform him from a boring academic into an exotic art historian. He could hold forth, and people would listen, even if they were only there to be in the orbit of Sandrine. She made him seem more stable, substantial. Having a beautiful, young French girlfriend who worked at the d'Orsay, impressed his superiors at the Gallery no end. He was good for Sandrine's career for the same reasons. In Paris, they seemed to fit into the arts clique seamlessly.

It could easily have happened the other way around, but it was through a contact of Louis' that Sandrine heard about a position at the National Portrait Gallery, and she moved to London and in with him.

Everything seemed to fit together so well. They were a perfect match so everyone said, including his mother. 'Don't let her get away Louis, you'll never find better than belle Sandrine,' she said.

Of course, Louis had been in relationships before. He had broken up with Hillary not long after meeting Sandrine. Actually she had left him. She said he was too self-centered. All his previous relationships seemed to end up the same way. None were satisfying not even with Zoe, who he had gone out with for years. He put it down to the constant studying, and research that he had to do to further his budding career. So it seemed that marrying Sandrine was the natural thing to do.

As Sandrine was younger than Louis, she wanted to wait to have children, and pursue her career. For years, they had been so wrapped up in their work that they spent less and less time with each other. Every now and then he would hear whispers or snide remarks about his too perfect relationship, with his too beautiful and too young trophy wife. But that was the way it was in London and Paris for that matter. People could be vicious, jealous.

The years sped by and eventually Sandrine was ready to have a child. Now Louis rather late in life was a father. He looked back at his relationship with Sandrine with affection. They were fond of each other. They had been good for each other, and had stayed together despite everything.

Louis pulled into the driveway of David's country mansion in the Chilterns just outside London. He hadn't asked David who else would be there. What did it matter anyway? It would be a couple of days with no responsibilities, and he was sure there would be no women for him to admire. It would just be the usual crew of aging, married friends of David.

David ran a hedge fund, and he was rich. Not exactly a boy, but even after all the years Louis had known him, he still behaved like one. Caterers had been arranged for the weekend with no expense spared, so David had promised.

He pulled into the long driveway and parked. As he opened his car door, he heard laughter and clinking of glasses. He made his way up the steps, and into the vestibule to be greeted by a waiter, and took a glass of champagne. He found an empty chair in the living room and sat down. It was mostly the usual group of old friends, but there were some new faces as well. A friend of David's from their university days sat to his left. Crashing old bore thought Louis. On his right was David's wife Anna, who was always charming and talkative.

Contented, detached, he nibbled hors d'oeuvres and sipped his drink without joining in the conversation. Across the room a couple he had not encountered before introduced themselves to those around them. The man was dark and a bit sombre. He spoke softly, his eyes looking downward as if embarrassed. Occasionally he became more animated and strident. He referred to his partner as, 'Darling Agata.'

Agata certainly is a darling, thought Louis. It was not that she was particularly good looking. She had a wide face with a strong jaw and a slender figure. She moved her hands animatedly. Wearing a moderately low cut top, her breasts moved pleasantly when she laughed. As she spoke earnestly, on import and learned subjects her blond hair danced around her shoulders. She had a strange accent, hard to place that only increased her allure. But it was her eyes, that were her best feature, blue, large and sparkling.

Agata looked Louis in the eye when speaking in his direction. Surprised, he moved his hand to cover his chin, is she talking to me? He now felt obliged to enter the conversation, and made an attempt to be charming. Certain he had failed to impress her, he redoubled his efforts. Several times she looked him straight in the eye, and asked him poignant questions about art, and politics. He was fascinated by her, but she was taken, or so it seemed.

Later on, Louis was drinking with several of the men in David's study. Undertones of machismo and bawdiness came to the fore as the men became increasingly intoxicated. David, his eyes reddened by the alcohol, asked Agata's partner, 'So what's she like Mark, you know, between the sheets?'

'She's not my girlfriend David,' he replied.

The men faces distorted in drunkenness winked at each other. 'I'll bet she's a tiger Mark eh? Go on you can tell us,' urged David to peels of laughter. But he received no further response from Mark, who looked sheepishly into his drink.

Not his girlfriend? So what is, 'darling Agata' to Mark? Louis wondered.

Dinner was to be served, and Louis took a random seat at the long table in the richly decorated dining room. The chair next him was empty and as if from nowhere, Agata appeared and sat down.

'Louis, I'm so glad you came for the weekend. I've met several of David's friends now but you're the most interesting so far,' she said, her eyes looking straight into his.

He nearly fell out of his seat. It was not her sudden appearance that shook him. No, he was astonished that she was interested in him at all, yet there were her big blue eyes, piercing him as if straight into his soul.

She cannot be interested in me, he thought. It's just the first time in years that I'm having a real conversation with a woman, that's all. Normally it's just polite, distant chit chat. I'm not used to someone like Agata talking to me in this way. She is just trying to be friendly, nothing more, he thought.

'Agata, that's nice. I'm glad to meet you as well. But tell me, where are you from? You have such an exotic accent.'

'I'm from Poland Louis, although I haven't lived there for years.'

Ah, Poland, that might explain it, he thought. She is so much more direct than the English women I work with and meet at gallery openings and formal occasions.

'How long have you been in London?'

'It's been nearly a year already. I was in the USA for many years, studying and working before coming here.'

'I guess that's why your accent is so different.'

'Yes, I mostly learned English in America.'

He thought it impolite to ask her age, but he judged her to be in her early thirties. 'What do you do Agata, for a living?'

'I'm a physicist'

'You must have spent many years studying?'

'Yes, it's true I have Physics and Computer Science degrees. My PhD took a lot of effort, but I enjoyed it. How about yourself, what did you study Louis?'

'Me, nothing really, you know, Art History. I just looked at pictures in books and went to museums.'

Mark sat down across the table from Louis. 'I think I had a one too many G&Ts darling Agata,' he said looking at the two of them. He turned his face to look directly at Louis, smiled and lowered his eyes.

'Well Mark, go easy on the wine with dinner eh? We have to get up early in the morning for the croquet game.'

'Yes darling, don't worry about me,' he murmured without raising his eyes.

Soon the dining room was filled with guests grabbing chairs and engaging in lively conversation. Agata was very popular; everyone wanted to talk to her. Giles, seated at the far end, shouted down the length of the table in an upper-class accent with everyone forced to listen in. She had a dry sense of humour and laughter reverberated around the table at her jokes. Louis was disappointed. He had barely spoken to her at all, and now he was just one small voice butting into the discussion. He gave up trying to impress her and faded into the background.

David had an exceptional wine cellar and the waiter diligently refilled Louis' glass as soon as it was half empty. Louis was enjoying himself now, lost in a drunken internal debate about the merits of the wines that had been served. He was sure he glimpsed Agata looking at him out of the corner of her eye several times, even though she wasn't talking to him.

After dinner, brandy was served. Louis swished his glass around, and took his first sip, Um, excellent Armagnac. Looking up he caught Agata in a full on stare. Her eyes danced away from his, embarrassed at having been caught admiring him. Mark was deeply engrossed in a conversation with the crashing bore, while Anna, who had swapped places and was now sitting opposite, smiled knowingly at Agata and Louis.

Recomposed, Agata asked, 'What part of town do you live in Louis?"

'Bayswater, you know, on the north side of Kensington Gardens.'

'Oh, not far from the Serpentine Gallery?'

'No, not far at all.'

'There's an exhibition on there at the moment that I would like to see. I was thinking of going during the week.'

My God, thought Louis, she wants me to take her.

'Really, what's the exhibition? I should know of course in my line of work, but I don't recall what's on there at the moment.'

'Yes Louis, you work at the National Gallery don't you?' asked Agata tilting her head to one side as if genuinely curious.

Anna didn't let Louis reply and butted in, 'Agata, I would love to go the Serpentine gallery, I haven't been there in ages. How about we go together?'

'Anna, yes, thanks, that would be lovely.'

'Wonderful, I'll call you on Monday and arrange it. I can't wait.'

Anna looked at Louis triumphant that she had foiled his chance of a tryst with Agata. Mark finished his conversation with the crashing bore, as David slapped Louis on the shoulder and declared, 'Everyone, time to take our brandies out onto the veranda.'

Louis lingered at the table hoping to be left alone with Agata as everyone left, but Anna whisked her away gushing, 'Agata, I have something wonderful to show you, come with me.'

He stayed as if stuck to his chair while he struggled to make sense of what had just happened. I know I'm a bit tipsy, but I'm sure Agata wants to see me, alone, away from Mark. I know that look, those glances. I may have been married for years, but I still remember how a girl looks at you when she wants you. Maybe I'm wrong, perhaps she's just flirtatious. But I'm going to find out one way or the other.

Determined, he stood up straight, pushed his fingers through his hair. He placed his left hand in his jacket pocket and with the best slight swagger he could muster, followed the boisterous party out into the late evening air.

After one o'clock Agata and Mark said goodnight and went upstairs to bed. Louis followed soon after. There was no point staying up if Agata was not there. His room was one of several on the first floor of the house. He glimpsed the two of them in the corridor ahead of him, and presumed they were going into the same room. Humph, so she is with Mark.

The next morning Louis was woken by a pigeon sitting on the window-sill cooing. Lying on his back in the morning light his mind meandered through the rooms of the National Gallery. I love birds, they make beautiful subjects for paintings. Funny how few birds there are in the Gallery. There are Zeus as an eagle in the *Rape of Ganymede* and *Leda and the Swan* of course. There are landscapes and mystical scenes that take place outside, lots of skies, water, trees, but few birds. Oh, mustn't forget flowers, there are plenty of them. Surprisingly, nudes are not as common as the general public imagine.

Stretching his arms and yawning he spoke out loud 'Well, no one is going to bring me a cup of coffee, so I had better go find one,' and he pushed aside the cover.

The dining room was now set for breakfast with trays of croissant, dishes of bacon, eggs, kedgeree and cereal laid out in a buffet. David stood peering into an empty bowl hung-over.

'No kippers?' enquired Louis.

David pulled a silver lid off a large serving dish to reveal a steaming heap of smoked fish. After a couple of cups of coffee, kippers and eggs, David and Louis were at last in a fit state to converse with each other.

'So David, How did you meet Agata and Mark?'

'Well, Mark works for us now. He brought expertise to the table, knowledge and skills that I do not possess. Cyber security is critical nowdays.'

'Ah, so he and Agata are important to you. I didn't really understand. I assumed they were just new acquaintances.'

'Mark is important if a somewhat left brain, you know what I mean. Agata, she is a force unto herself.'

Anna burst into the room full of enthusiasm unwelcome after so much alcohol the night before. 'Happy birthday David!' she hugged her husband.

Louis had entirely forgotten about his friend's anniversary but shook David's hand with as much vigour as he could. Moments later, Agata came in from the garden. 'David, Anna, come on, the game has started.'

A littlie reluctantly David followed the two women out into the garden. Louis relieved at having been left alone, helped himself to more kippers. Agata, returned with a smile. She paused, and looked Louis in the eye,

'Come on, you must join us as my special guest. We're going to play croquet.'

She held out her hand. Louis placed his trembling fingers on hers, and she led him out to the lawn.

'Who invited him?' said Mark

'I did', said Agata, smiling, confidently.

From that moment on Louis ceased to care what Mark or anyone else thought about him and his darling Agata. He was enchanted. More importantly, he was invited. Agata had expressly invited him to be with her.

Louis did his best to play croquet, as did everyone else. The only person who seemed to actually enjoy the game was Agata. But everyone made an effort. Just after noon, Agata finally yawned and looked at her phone to check the time.

She said, 'Oh my, I think last night is beginning to catch up with me. Maybe it's time for a lie down before lunch. What to you think Mark?'

'Yes darling, a pre-siesta siesta, perfect idea,' he replied.

They all headed to their bedrooms for a much-needed nap. Louis followed behind Agata and Mark again, but sober this time, he paused as he reached his room, and noticed that they went into two separate rooms adjacent to each other. He pushed the door open and flopped on the bed. My goodness, she's not sleeping with him after all. He smiled, and lay on his back with his hands behind his head.

He dosed off for a few minutes but was woken by a tap tap in the corridor. He stood up, creaked open his door and peered up the hallway. Giles was standing there as Agata greeted him, 'Giles, come on in,' she said as her arm came out and pulled Giles into her room by the waist and quickly closed the door.

Agata with Giles, what's going on? He went to his window which looked out onto the lawn strewn with croquet hoops and opened it. He leant out and strained to listen. Sure enough, her window was open and he just could just hear Agata's laugh and animated talking. A feeling of uncertainty engulfed him as if his life was now threatened. He sat on the bed and rubbed his chin. Either she's having it off with everyone, or no one. I wonder which it is.

At one thirty lunch was announced with a gong. Louis heard doors open, and people make their way from their rooms out to the veranda for another round of communal feasting. He looked out his window and saw Mark on the lawn, smoking a cigarette. Agata's door opened, and he heard her and Giles walk down the hall and stairs.

He followed them but continued on past the veranda into the garden to where Mark was taking a long drag on his cigarette. 'Want one Louis?' he said.

'Oh no, but thanks, I've never smoked cigarettes.'

Mark shrugged, looked at his shoes and took another drag.

'So how long have you and Agata known each other Mark?'

'Not long, about three months. My parents are Polish, although I was brought up in London. I guess we hit it off right away. We have a lot of things in common.'

'Have you spent much time in Poland?'

'Only when I was in the army. I was mostly in Germany, but I used to visit a lot.'

'The army?'

'Yeah, you know how it goes. Straight out of school, it was more like an apprenticeship.'

'Are you out of the army now?'

'Oh yes, it's a young mans game you know. We're all sent out to pasture before we become old and decrepit. I did get a medal from the Queen though.'

'David said you are in business together now.'

'Well, I look after security for the firm.'

Agata called out, 'Come on you two, champagne!'

Mark stubbed his cigarette into the lawn, and they went back to the veranda. Louis found a seat at the far end of the table from Agata, Mark and Giles. Puzzled by their relationship to each other he quietly watched and listened to them. The three of them talked earnestly together all afternoon. But all the same, occasionally, Louis caught Agata looking at him with her piercing eyes.

Intrigued by her now, and not a little frightened of Mark, he could not square him with Agata at all. Mark and Agata have a lot in common? They don't have anything in common. She's a PhD and he's a squaddie. Perhaps Agata was just looking for friends when she arrived in London, any harbour in a storm. But whatever it was they had or have it won't last. What about Giles? He's a buffoon, a Hooray Henry. No Louis assured himself. Someone is going to end up with Agata, but it's not going to be Mark or Giles.

The rest of the day was a blur of champagne and brandy with birthday cake and a conga line through the garden after midnight. On Monday morning, Louis had no recollection of how or when he made it to bed. However he woke up as normal, his clothes neatly folded on the bedside chair.

Driving back to London he found a piece of paper in his pocket. He now remembered exchanging email addresses with Agata before going to bed and his heart pounded with excitement. Turning up the radio and increasing his speed, he drove straight home back to his beautiful family.

3

The next day Louis looked up the website for the Serpentine Gallery. The current exhibition was a series of nightmarish drawings of dogs wearing highly coloured knitted sweaters by an artist called Golub Leonus. Good grief, she can't possibly want to see this. He wrote an email to Agata.

> Hi Agata, It was very nice to meet you on the weekend. The Serpentine is showing an exhibition of Golub Leonus. Is that the one you were interested to see? In any case, if you ever need a tour guide for the National Gallery I would be happy to show you around.
> Take care,
> Louis

He took his time to review it before sending, his finger hovered over the mouse button. He didn't want to come on too strong, rather he thought, It's best to underplay it. Just send her something she can respond to, and then we can have an online conversation to get things going. He wanted to invite her out, but if she said no, then that would be the end of it. So instead he included a semi invitation that could be taken either way, open-ended. Satisfied, he clicked the send button and tried to forget about Agata until he received a reply.

Fortunately, the remainder of the week was taken up by a series of planning meetings. During breaks, he hurried back to his office to check his email. Friday afternoon came around, but he had received nothing from Agata. Disappointed he picked up his book and walked across Trafalgar Square to the Charring Cross tube and home.

The following Monday at work was peaceful. Far too peaceful, and Louis clicked his send/receive button constantly hoping for a reply from Agata to suddenly appear. On Tuesday, he was beginning to give up hope until, a little tab from his email popped up - message received. His finger fumbled the mouse as he opened it.

> Louis! The days are flying by. I intended to drop you a line sooner, but a paper I'm writing has taken up all my free time. I have to go to Charring Cross Road near the National Gallery for an appointment tomorrow afternoon. I only have an hour to spare, but perhaps you could take me on the tour you mentioned? I guess you are going to the party this weekend? Hope to see you there.
> Agata.

He read the email over and over again. Slowly he typed a short reply. Seconds later he had a date with Agata from 2-3 pm on the next day.

In the morning he left home with a spring in his step. He forgot his book and didn't notice anyone on the train. He flew up the steps of the gallery jauntily and said a merry hello to all the staff, his left hand not in his pocket, but waving by his side. Emily gave him a peculiar look as he said, 'Emily delightful morning isn't it?' with a beaming smile on his face.

He sat in his office without moving until five minutes to two. Then he pushed out into the stream of people and made his way to the Espresso Bar. It was a good place to meet people who were unfamiliar with the gallery. He stood at the entrance and at exactly two o'clock Agata walked up and smiled.

'Agata, how good to see you, would you like a coffee?'

'No thanks Louis, too many already today.'

'Alright, well let's begin the tour, come with me.'

Louis put on his best professional air, which came naturally to him as he had taken hundreds of people through the gallery over the years, including his wife when she first visited him in London. 'The collection has over 2,300 works, with many priceless paintings including Velázquez's *Toilet of Venus* and Van Gogh's *Sunflowers*. We'll have a look at these, but let's start with Titian.'

With his left hand in his jacket pocket, he led Agata up the stairs, through the Central Hall into room 2 and stopped in front of Titian's *Bacchus and Ariadne*.

He Began, 'Paintings at that time often told an elaborate story. Nowadays we are more used to narratives being unfolded in moving images with sound, or by reading. In the past people were more comfortable than we are today at seeing a whole story in a static painting. This one tells the story, in a poetic way, of Ariadne, and the wine god Bacchus who fell in love with her at first sight.'

He took his left hand out of his pocket and pointed at Bacchus, 'Notice the stars in the sky above Ariadne...'

He glanced at Agata and realised that she was looking at his left hand and his wedding ring. Louis closed his fingers and put his hand back in his pocket. He felt his wedding ring and rolled it round and round. 'It's just a sentimental thing that's all,' he murmured unable to look at Agata.

Flustered he continued on as best he was able. Usually, he could talk endlessly about all the paintings in the gallery, but now his confidence was gone and in a perfunctory manner he led her from room to room fumbling his words all the way. They looked at *The Madonna of the Pinks*, by Raphael, Leonardo's Cartoon, paintings by Vermeer, Velázquez, van Gogh.

When they reached the rooms with the impressionists and post-impressionists, Agata became more interested. They paused for a long time at *After the Bath*, by Degas.

'Late in his career Degas began to draw women bathing and combing their hair. This one is a drawing of a woman sitting on a chair beside a bathtub, drying herself with a towel. Do you like it Agata?'

'Yes, this is my favorite so far. Somehow it is the most intimate. So many of the others we have looked at seem over staged, too well thought out perhaps.'

'Degas was famous for his meticulous composition and planning, but he more than likely watched this woman take a bath and then did an initial sketch which gives it a feeling of spontaneity.'

'I wonder what they talked about while she was bathing.'

'I don't know, but you can see how much he loves her form, her skin. It's sumptuous, full of texture and blurred lines that give a sense of movement.'

'Do you think he made love with this woman?'

'Perhaps, although probably not. He was intensely professional about his work. I think like all of the artists we have seen today, what he most loved was the beauty of the form, light, colour. Somehow they wanted to capture something of the vibrancy of life.'

'Capture it, own it,' she said with a bitter note to her voice.

'I think not in that sense, more that they wanted to preserve the moment, somehow keep the scene. Life is transient, fleeting. We all suffer the ravages of time, nothing lasts. I think they were trying to hold onto life.'

'I think that's where my interest in physics came from, a wish to understand the transience of the world, to piece together the history of life.'

'Isn't physics about the non-living world?' Louis asked.

'No, physics *is* the living world. The universe is made of matter, things, stuff. It is the way matter interacts, its elemental particles and the interrelationships between everything else that is the living world. Like a spider's web, pull a thread on the farthest edge and the vibrations are felt all across the weave.'

'And God is the spider?"

'Ah, God, that is something outside of my field,' she smiled.

'I think that artists, all artists throughout the ages are trying to put their finger on God, to stop God from moving around, to freeze God so we can say for sure that it's real.'

'That is an interesting idea, similar to quantum mechanics where objects only exist in a haze of probability. They have a certain chance of being at point A, another chance of being at point B and so on. You can't put your finger on it, stop it from moving. One instant it could be a wave, the next a particle or nothing at all.'

'So you don't discount the existence of God?'

'No, why should I. Our understanding of the universe is incomplete. We are like kindergarten children; we know practically nothing about the universe or existence.'

'Ah, what about the wisdom of eastern mysticism, philosophy, religion? Perhaps human knowledge is greater than the modern world acknowledges.'

'I am more interested in the real world, the one we live in rather than the one we imagine.'

'You're an existentialist! But is not the world we live in - the human condition - our collective imagination?'

'I'm not really an existentialist. I do expect that there are underlying universal principles to the structure to the universe. Perhaps we see the world from a unique viewpoint, and that is who we are. But we exist now, here, and that is what we must deal with. But you are a romantic I think?'

'Maybe I am a romantic, stuck in the nineteenth century. I do believe that the most important thing for an artist is to express their feelings, and not be bound by artificial rules.'

They moved on to the next room and the *Bathers at Asnières*, by Georges Seurat.

'This one is more like applied science, he seems to have defined the shapes by light alone. Somehow it doesn't seem painted,' said Agata.

'Yes, it is interesting the way he depicts the effects of light and atmosphere. Do you like this one?'

'I'm not sure, it gives a very vibrant effect, but the people...'

'I think he was after simplicity of form. The people in the painting, they are together sitting by the river, or bathing in it. It's a communal scene...'

'Yet they are not looking at each other. Their eyes are hidden from each other and us the viewers. It's a strange painting.'

'Your eyes, I mean, the way you look at me, with your lovely eyes. Most paintings of people don't show the subject looking at the viewer. Sometimes they gaze into the distance,' said Louis.

'Mostly people don't look you in the eye, they are afraid. They don't want to give too much away,' said Agata.

'But you look me in the eye Agata, as if you can see into my heart.'

'I always look people in the eye.'

'Do you like what you see?'

'You look nice, interesting, but I can't really see into your heart.'

'Oh, the way you looked at me I thought you might find me attractive.'

'Looks aren't what make me want to be with a man. It's a spark about them, some sensibility that reaches me.'

'Do I have a spark?'

'Maybe, but you are so reserved it makes it hard for me to see the man behind the mask. What about your likes, what attracts you to a woman?'

'It's the same for me I think. There has to be a certain something, almost indefinable, the qualities you see in some of the great paintings,

Rubens, Raphael, Leonardo and Picasso.'

'Wow, what high standards you have!'

'I don't mean they have to be a great beauty, it's the subtle quality that somehow the artist captures in time and space that lives on, their essence.'

'For you, are paintings a substitute for real life? They are things in the past gone. No vibration on the spider's web will reach the women you see in paintings. I'm flesh and blood, real, alive. You can't love an ideal, an essence. You must love a person. Their good points bad points, the woman.'

'You want me to love you?'

'We were talking about art Louis.'

'Are you in love with someone?'

'Maybe, maybe not, that's personal, for me and the one I love.'

'Agata, you and Mark, are you together?'

'No, no we're not. He has it in his head that I love him. I like him as a friend, but he has become a bit obsessed with me, that's all. I always seem to be surrounded by crazy people.'

'What about Giles?'

'Oh Giles, don't be silly. He's just a friend like you are Louis. We're friends aren't we?'

She looked at him with the hint of a tear in her eye. She peered into his eyes and he moved his face towards hers. She turned away and said, 'I have to go to my appointment now. Three o'clock, I'm already late.'

She walked towards the doorway, half turned and waved goodbye.

Louis looked at the Seurat and felt that he, like the painting was stuck in time. She had gone and left him in a state of suspension.

He neglected to ask her about the party and he had no idea whose it was or where it was going to be. Ah ha, David will know. He called David while walking back to his office.

'David, we haven't spoken since your party. It was a fun weekend.'

'All a bit of a blur for me I'm afraid. I vaguely remember a conga line and a game of croquet, ' David replied.

'I must say that the weekend was a tonic for me. I haven't been socially active for years as you know. I got a bit of a taste for parties in fact. I don't suppose there is anything happening this weekend?'

'Louis, you're wondering if there is a party this weekend?'

'Just wondering, in case there is, you know...'

'You want to go a party? Funnily enough, there is a party this weekend.'

'Oh really, where?'

'Belgravia, you remember Giles? He was at my birthday. Anyway, he is having a do on Saturday night. Do you want to come with me?'

'If it's OK if I meet you there? I'll have to see when I can get away from the family. You know, pop out for an hour or so.'

'Right, 53 Chester Square, see you there.'

4

On Saturday evening, he waited until Sandrine had gone to bed, snuck out of the apartment and took the tube from Bayswater to Sloane Square. As he walked the short distance to Chester Square, his nerves began to fray. What am I going to say to everyone? What will David think? He knows I don't go to parties. As soon as he sees me with Agata he'll know what's happening. In fact, I'm sure he had figured it out before I hung up the phone.

What a fool I am. Regardless, I think Agata wants me. This might be just my wild imagination, but I can tell that she feels for me, he thought.

No I can't! I haven't the foggiest idea whether she fancies me or not. I can't divine her thoughts. All I know is how women look in paintings, their eyes turning inwards expressing something that neither I nor anyone else will ever grasp. But I can't let this go on past this night. I must find out tonight, one way or another, does she desire me or not?

He walked with his hands stuffed into his pockets and his shoulders hunched. Almost involuntarily, he slipped his wedding ring off his finger and left it loose in his pocket.

As soon as Louis turned into the leafy square he could hear laughter and clinking glasses. One of the five-story terraces was ablaze with lights and people were visible through the windows that were open to the warm summer air. He pushed his way past a couple smoking on the front porch and through the front door. He helped himself to a glass of wine from a drinks table in the front room.

Looking for Agata, he went down the stairs to the basement and walked along the hallway. He grasped the edge of an open doorway, and turned his head into a brightly lit room. Radiant, happy, holding forth, Agata was sitting on a sofa with Giles and David.

A pang of uncontrollable fear took hold of him. Stepping backward into the shadow of the hallway he felt unable to move fighting his instinct to flee. He could not bear the thought of facing David and Giles. Agata, framed by the open doorway tossed her head back in a laugh. He withdrew into himself, unsure.

After a few moments, calmness came over him. Agata was talking and waving her hands, her eyes full of passion. Seeing only her, he stepped out into the light. She looked in his direction, and a smile moved across her face as their eyes met.

Louis walked into the room and reaching her looked down at her upturned face, he pushed his hand forward towards her's and Agata moved her fingers into his. He enclosed them and pulled at her hand. She stood up, and their lips embraced. Without speaking, he led her out of the room and up the stairs.

They pushed past a group of people sitting on the steps. Louis held her hand firmly and they continued up until they arrived at the top floor. Looking down the corridor he saw an empty bedroom with no light on but the door ajar. He led her inside and closed the door behind them. In the darkness without speaking they embraced, kissed, and Louis cupped her breast.

Seconds later a loud knock on the door startled them. Their eyes were adjusting to the darkness with light spreading in from the window. Louis looked at Agata and motioned her to stand aside out of view while he opened the door.

Mark, his face red demanded, 'Is Agata with you? She was seen coming up here.'

'No Mark, look, I'm just a bit dizzy, drunk and I need to lie down for a moment,' and he closed the door with a bang. Mark stamped on the floor outside and shuffled his feet noisily, 'Agata, come out for fucks sake.'

Louis moved Agata towards the bed and motioned her to sit down. He whispered in her ear, 'Do you want to go with him?'

'No,' she said shaking her head.

'Is he your lover?'

'No, I told you, he's obsessed with me, I can't shake him.'

He held her hand and kissed her moist lips. He felt sure now, she did want him and he would abandon everything for her, surrender himself to her. He moved her to lie down. She pressed her body to his as if afraid to let go. They kissed but after a few moments she inched her face away from his and resisted his hands, uncertain now.

That idiot Mark interrupted the perfect moment; she was going to give herself to me, thought Louis. He changed tack and began to whisper sweet nothings softly in her ear.

'It was your eyes, the way you looked at me, I knew you wanted me, you do want me, you know it, let yourself go. Everything will be alright. I feel so much for you, darling...'

'Yes, but you are married, she said,'

Their hands entwined she searched his fingers for his ring. When she didn't feel it, she withdrew back into herself a little more. 'You're a liar, she whispered.'

'I'm not, I like you a lot, I don't know where it's all going, but we have tonight, let's follow our passion.'

'Sometimes you wear a wedding ring, sometimes not, you're a liar.'

'Don't worry about my stupid ring, sentimental that's all, I told you.'

'So where is your wife?'

'Forget about her, she's away, she went home, that's that.'

'Just for a few weeks?'

'No, no, months. What can I do, what can I say. I'm here with you. I didn't plan to fall for you, nor you me.'

'I like you Louis, you're interesting, we can just be friends.'

'You can never be friends with one that you desire, or who desires you.'

'Oh, some friend you are, blackmailing me.'

'No, I'm just saying, it's true, afterwards, after a couple make love, then they're intimate and can be friends. Until then it is impossible no matter how much they like each other, all their being is full of tension, unfulfilled desire.'

'So you're saying that we can never be friends because we are attracted to each other, but we have to make love so we can become friends?'

'Yes, it's an illogical, unreasonable situation. So what are we to do? I think that as we want each other we should make love, and take it from there.'

'We can't just make love here, in someone else's room with Mark prowling around.'

'Then come away with me, we can leave right now.'

'Louis, don't be ridiculous, you have a wife, and I have my life here I can't just run away with you.'

'Just for a few days, so we can get to know each other and see where this goes. Come with me right now. We can spend the night at the Cadogan Hotel a short walk from here. Tomorrow we'll take the train to Paris and stay at the Pavillon de la Reine, for just a few days then we'll see.'

'Those hotels sound expensive.'

'They are, very expensive indeed. The Pavillion is an exquisite hotel in the best part of Paris where all the highest class Haute couture and jewellery shops are. The hotel restaurant is world famous. Of course, we'll also have the whole of Paris to enjoy. We'll have a fabulous, romantic time. '

'I have to work on Monday.'

'You can take a few days off, personal reasons, they won't mind.'

'Saying personal reasons is better than sick as that would be untrue.'

'Exactly, so it will be fine. Come on let's go, now.'

'Do you know Paris well?'

'Yes, nearly as well as I know London. My mother is from Paris.'

'Oh, so that's where you got the name Louis?'

'Yes, I'm named after my Grandfather, not King Louis don't worry. I can show you all the secret romantic places in Paris. Places tourists never see.'

'You know, I've not been to Paris. I went straight from university in Warsaw to post graduate studies at Harvard. I'm more at home in the USA than in Europe.'

'I can't wait to hear all about it, darling. But I don't hear Mark outside anymore. So let's stand up now and we can walk to the Cadogan. Isn't this exciting?'

He stood up and pulled her arm to lift her off the bed, but she resisted. She pulled his hand back and made him lie next to her again. They lay in silence. Louis moved his lips to her earlobe and kissed her.

He whispered, 'Agata, we didn't plan this. I just walked into David's house and there you were. I had no idea I was going to meet you, fall for you. But I did meet you and I know you fell for me.'

'I'm falling alright, but no Louis, I can't go away with you. You can never be serious with me, you have a wife.'

'You don't know my situation. I'm free to be with you, and here we are tonight, together, full of desire, we will never be here again, open up, take me, now, tonight.'

'Louis, I hear you, but if this is real it will last a bit of time. I need to think, to reflect on what you've said. Let me think it over. I must go now.'

'Agata, just relax and wait a while. There's no hurry, we can keep talking.'

She pushed her arm against the bed to stand up, but Louis resisted and gently stopped her. Her eyes tightened, angry now.

'Stay, stay with me now, I won't do anything, just lie down and keep talking to me.'

'You won't do anything, sure. No, I'm going now.'

'Agata, this is our night, here we are together now, hold me close, stay with me.'

'So you don't care about your wife?'

'Of course I do, but I care more about you, us. Don't worry about my wife, she's not in the frame any more. It's something I have to sort out. I want to be with you.'

Agata stood up, resolute, and moved towards the door. Turning to look at him, she said, 'We can talk again tomorrow.'

'Agata, tonight belongs to us, try and understand. Will you come away with me?'

'Maybe I'll go to Paris with you, give me tonight to think about it.'

Agata closed the door behind her leaving Louis as if in a vacuum, in space, alone.

He lay on the bed, mon Dieu, he thought, I wasn't wrong, she does want me, she does. He was elated, but a sense of failure enveloped him. He opened the door and made his way quickly down the stairs and walked straight out the front door of the house. He bumped into Mark who was smoking a cigarette and nearly knocked him over.

'Mark, so sorry I didn't see you.'

'It's alright Louis, where's Agata?'

'I just have to make a call, I'll be back soon.'

'Where is she?' he shouted after him.

Louis walked as briskly as he could to the corner of the square and turned left into Eccleston Street. He barely stopped, even for traffic until he reached the safety of home. His wife was asleep as he crept into bed. He reached out to touch her, but pulled his hand back. Curling himself into a ball, he gathered the covers over his head and closed hie eyes.

5

The next morning he awoke to the sound of his baby crying. Sandrine came into the room and picked up petite Julie, and carried her downstairs. How mysterious, Sandrine is, with her unknowable smile, like the most famous painting in the world, he pondered. Maybe that is her uniqueness. What goes on inside her head, her heart? I see so much in her face, but I don't know if what I see is real, correct. I don't know what her desires are, except to work, raise our daughter and love me too. Is that enough, all? I don't think I have ever understood.

He turned over to lie down again and the memory of the night before returned. Agata, oh my, how could you slip my mind even for a moment? My flirtation is over, thank goodness. Yes she does desire me, that's all I needed to know. But why did she pull away from me? How could I be so near, so close to her but fail to win her?

He pulled himself out of bed and went downstairs for breakfast. Glancing at the kitchen clock he saw it was late, he had slept in.

Agata said she would think about my proposal and we would talk again today. What if she calls me? She doesn't have my number. David might give it to her, what if Sandrine answers? David won't give her the landline stupid! Still, I had better call her.

Louis didn't have Agata's phone number, just her email address. He logged into his email and found her message to him and was relieved that she had included her number at the bottom. He couldn't call her from home so he put on his jacket and opened the front door. 'Darling, I'll be back soon,' he shouted to Sandrine.

He walked around the corner to Moscow Road and the Byzantium Cafe and sat down at a table. 'Espresso please,' he called to the waitress.

What am I going to say to Agata? Fear crept over him like a chill wind. I failed last night, mercifully. What if she had said yes, and we had just woken up at the Cadogan? I would be calling a cab to go to Saint Pancras station to catch the Eurostar to Paris. On the way there I would have to call the Pavillon de la Reine to make a reservation. That hotel costs an absolute fortune! My god, I would be paying off my credit card for the next ten years. Do I even have enough credit for one night there? What was I thinking? He felt desperate for a cigarette even though he had never smoked in his life.

His coffee arrived and he put a lump of sugar in and stirred it with his teaspoon, then another lump, then another, stirring vigorously. 'Would you like some coffee with your sugar, love?' the waitress laughed.

Louis picked up his tiny cup and threw the viscous lukewarm liquid in the back of his throat. His fingers began tapping the table like playing drums. I haven't done that since I was twelve. He remembered his mother chiding him as if he were a digging with a jackhammer, 'Arrête le marteau pneumatique garçon méchant!'

The coffee helped to calm him down and his thoughts began to coalesce. OK, she'll decide no and that will be that. What if she says yes? She won't, she's not stupid. She must know I'm mad. She'll think that I'd say anything to get her into bed, and of course she's right. That fool Mark, if only he hadn't come looking for her like a lunatic. I would be in bliss, right now, with Agata in my arms!

He stood up and paced around the cafe. The waitress looked at him nervously and the only other customer left hurriedly. 'Are you alright sir?' she asked.

'Schhh, I'm thinking,' he barked.

He sat back down. Bliss, agony, bliss agony, either way there would have been much agony. I could not have stayed with Agata. I would have hurt her, hurt Sandrine, hurt myself. But I would have risked it all to be with her, I would have done it, I would be on that train now. Who knows where I would have ended up?

He reached for his phone in his jacket pocket but felt his wedding ring instead. He slipped it back on his finger and found the phone in his other pocket.

'Hi, it's Louis, how are you today?'

'Louis, I'm OK I guess,' replied Agata.

'How is Mark?'

'Mark? Oh, I don't know I haven't seen him.'

'It's just, you know, he was looking for you.'

'Yes, he kept looking for me alright.'

'He did? Oh, crikey, well um...'

'All the men I know seem to be unhinged, don't worry I'm used to it.'

'Well I'll never act crazy, I promise you that.'

'You, not act crazy?'

Louis paused, and asked, 'Are we OK, Agata, you and I?'

'Yeah, sure, no problem with me.'

Louis felt unease in Agata that he was not expecting, 'Agata what are your plans for today?'

'Well, I don't know, you suggested a lot of things last night, but I don't really know you, so you know ...'

'Ah well, I understand, of course, you don't know me it's true.'

'So I don't know, I can't just, you know...'

'No, no of course not, it was silly of me to think, no, needless to say, I understand. So, enjoy the rest of your weekend.'

'Oh, alright then Louis, of course we can still go to the Serpentine I suppose?'

'The Serpentine, of course, call me whenever you want to go I'd love that, sure. So, goodbye now.'

'OK, goodbye.'

Once again, Louis asked himself, what just happened? Did I ditch her or did she ditch me? I hope it was she that ended it, because hell hath no fury as that of a woman scorned.

Uncertain, as if something was missing, he still felt relieved. So did the waitress when he paid for his coffee and left. He went home to his beautiful wife and lovely baby and acted as if nothing had ever happened, except, that during the day a feeling of heaviness and loss came over him.

Holding his baby distracted him, but when he put her down, the memory of Agata's eyes came back to him. What did she mean when she said, '... he kept looking for me alright.' Did Mark eventually find her? I was not terribly brave. I didn't make sure she got home, just left the party.

What did she mean when she said, 'You, not act crazy?' So she thought my insane pleading was crazed? She really does know what an idiot I am! She seemed pensive, uneasy. No, I know now, she wanted me to take her to Paris, that's it. Last night I was so ardent, and today I backed off completely. I made no effort to persuade her, I didn't even have any words of love for her. So she does feel scorned. She does think it was me who dumped her.

Oh no, what will she do now? I spurned her, she hates me. She demurred and went home not prepared to give in so easily, but was eager and waiting for me to continue my advances and what happened? The coward I am, I ran away.

Louis hands and shoulders began shuddering. He lay down on the bed feeling ill in his stomach. What will she do to me now? She'll denounce me for sure. She'll say terrible things against me. I'll lose my wife, my baby, my career, I'm destroyed.

On Monday, he ran up the steps of the gallery. He forgot to nod good morning to the staff. He hurried into his office without even noticing lovely Emily. His swagger was gone with his left hand flapping like a rope dangling in the wind. Distracted, he put off returning phone calls and emails. After lunch, he sat down again at his computer and wrote to Agata.

> Agata, it was nice to see you at the weekend. I am
> looking forward to going to the Serpentine Gallery with
> you. Let me know when you want to go. Best, L

Louis read the email before sending it. He wanted to let her know that he had not actually dumped her but was still interested in her. Humm, nothing controversial there, click, he sent it.

He waited nervously all week, desperate for a reply. If only she would respond and let me off the hook. Why does she torture me like this? Please email me so I know everything will be alright. We can have a coffee and a chat and be friends. But no email ever came.

The weekend arrived and Louis moped around the house. Sandrine became worried about him, 'Are you ill cheri?'

'I'm fine, just tired after a hard week nothing more.'

Wild scenarios engulfed him. He could think of nothing except how Agata could hurt him, but surely she won't? If only she would reply to my email with a kind word he lamented. He imagined her talking to David, '... he's not just married, he has a four-month-old baby.'

What on earth must she think of me? She'll set Mark onto me, a soldier, security. Oh my, he was probably SAS, why else would he have received a medal from the Queen? He imagined innumerable ways that Agata would take her revenge upon him, with Mark as her henchman.

Back at work on Monday, he sat tapping his desk with his fingers. I cannot write another email to Agata. If she hasn't replied to the first one, I must not write to her again. He was determined to keep his dignity and not act in desperation. 'Damn it!' he shouted reaching for his keyboard.

> Agata, I hope that you and Mark are going along
> well? Let me know, I would love to hear your news.
> Coffee, exhibition? Whenever you're free. Louis

To hell with it, click, sent.

As the week progressed, his composure gradually returned, as much from exhaustion as anything else. On Friday afternoon just as he was about to leave for the weekend - message received - popped onto his screen.

> Louis, let's go the Serpentine Gallery tomorrow if
> you are free. A
> Agata, OK but meet me at the Serpentine Bar &
> Kitchen at the end of the lake. We can have a coffee
> before the exhibition. Is noon OK with you? L

He couldn't bear the thought of going to the Golub Leonus exhibition. A soon as he sent the reply he thought, why did I say noon? I'll never hold out until then. I should have said ten or nine. In any case, he now had an appointment with Agata. At last he could relax a bit. He went home feeling as if he had been through a wringer every day for the last two weeks.

He could not pace up and down his living room any longer without increasing Sandrine's already deep suspicion, so he left home at 10am and walked to Serpentine Kitchen. He found a table outside on the terrace with a view over the lake and ordered an espresso.

There were many ducks and geese paddling in the water. Fisherman on the bank lounged back in their chairs waiting for a bite. It was a warm day and bathers lolled about in the water of the Lido swimming area and sunbathed on the shore. A slight breeze made small ripples on the water. Puffy white clouds floated overhead creating shadows, dappled light then brilliant sunshine and back to shadows. The scene was reminiscent of the Seurat,

Bathers at Asnières, in the Gallery. He dozed off in the sunshine and Agata startled him when she arrived.

'Louis Louis!' she raised her voice as she sat down.

'Agata, how nice to see you, I arrived a while ago and was enjoying the view.'

'It's beautiful. I have not been here before, so peaceful.'

'How have you been Agata?'

'Busy, you know. Sorry I didn't get back to you sooner. To be honest, I didn't know what to say to you.'

'Are you mad at me?'

'Mad at you, no. I wonder about you though. What you are about, what you were thinking.'

'I don't believe there was any logical thought behind my actions or words actually. It all came from my Gallic heart.'

'The things you said to me, then you brushed me aside.'

'Did I? I didn't mean to. I became frightened I think.'

'Frightened of me?'

'I was frightened of the situation, frightened for myself in truth.'

'Ah, at last, some honesty from you.'

'Was I so dishonest with you?'

'It was hard for me to think that you really cared about me at all.'

'That is the one thing that is true Agata, I fell for you, I was afraid to say it to you, but I felt love for you. I would have gone all the way for you.'

'But only for a few hours, then you would have returned home to your, family, your baby.'

'No, no, not just a few hours. I would have given everything for you.'

'Everything? That would not have been right. What do you think I am? I don't want to ruin your life.'

'Why did you, I mean, you knew that I was married, why did you let me get close to you?'

'I don't know Louis, I liked you. I just followed my heart, or maybe it was my body. I was attracted to you. I felt something for you, but I realised too late that you are taken already.'

'When did you find out about my baby?'

'I hadn't asked David about you before, but I felt a bit despondent after you hung up, and I called him. We met later in the day.'

'I guess I pre-empted your answer. I never found out what you would have said. Would you have gone to Paris with me?'

'When you called I didn't know what I would say. I expected more from you. Maybe I would have gone away with you, but you seemed to have changed your mind. Now I know, you were only playing with me.'

'I wasn't playing with you. I'm not used to the attention of a beautiful woman like you. I didn't know how to behave.'

'You seem so sophisticated as if you're in control.'

'It's all a disguise, I'm sorry to say. Underneath I'm a writhing mess of fear and inadequacy.'

'I'm the same, I assure you.'

'I keep asking, but what about Mark? Did you see him that night after you left me in the room?'

'Yes, yes, he found me downstairs. We had an argument, it was horrible.'

'I'm sorry, I feel a coward. I should have done something.'

'Oh, it's alright it wasn't your fault. I hate anything clinging to me, and he tries to suffocate me. Ever since I left Poland, I've met nothing but psychotic men.'

'That's a bit strong, regarding me at least, I think.'

'Well, neurotic then. It was the same in America. I met guys who wanted too much, too little or were just too weird. That was one of the reasons I took the job in London. I would like to meet someone special, someone to care for me. Since I arrived, there was Mark. He was nice at first. But then he became so possessive, following me, checking up on me even after I broke it off with him. Then Giles, who's like a little child. He needs a mother, not a lover. David is different ...'

'David no?'

'At least it's not complicated with him. He only wants one thing and is quite up front about it.'

'Of course, I suppose it makes sense.'

'Then there is you Louis. What can I say about you?'

'That you forgive me, that you still like me.'

'Oh I forgive you, don't worry. Maybe I should go back to Poland. There the men are normal at least.'

'We can be friends can't we Agata?'

'You're the one who said lovers can't be friends.'

'Actually, I said we couldn't be friends until we became lovers.'

'Well, we didn't become lovers, did we?' said Agata.

'Apart from a few stolen kisses. Could we try again? I won't be so foolish this time.'

'No Louis, as you said we only had that one night. I think you just wanted to collect me, put me in your exhibition, hang me up.'

'I'm not like that Agata. I have no trophies.'

'No? Your wife, is she not just part of your collection? If not, how could you think of replacing her so easily?'

Louis lowered his face unable to answer. Had he wanted to replace Sandrine? Did David and Agata know him better than he knew himself? Perhaps they were the ones catagorising, sorting, putting people in pigeon holes, curating.

He watched a Canada goose as it paddled along the lake's edge. He raised his eyes, slowly. Like a canvas spread out before him, he gradually took in the whole scene attempting to divine the message the artist was trying to convey.

An old gentleman walked slowly down the lake shore towards the Lido with a cane and a boater hat. Two ladies, arm in arm strolled towards him bowing a greeting as they passed. Children splashed in the water while their parents looked on from the shore, talking amongst themselves. A young woman on a towel with a book was talking to a young man a short distance away sitting on his towel. A couple in rowboat stroked lazily along, talking and giggling. The breeze caught the full grown summer leaves in the trees which rustled distantly. The smell of cut lawn and roses filled the air in a sweet mix evocative of days gone by.

Such a civilised scene, he thought. Everyone was courteous, exchanging pleasantries, interested in each other. In the Seurat they were too introspective, only thinking about themselves. Not as Agata said, 'Like a spider's web, pull a thread on the farthest edge and the vibrations are felt all across the weave.'

Louis looked around. Agata had gone, he was alone. He felt detached from the web. He couldn't feel its vibrations; only look from afar. Like a viewer, outside the frame.

****

No.3

The Painter

1

The painter had been living in De Pijp district of Amsterdam for many years. For the last few years, he slept and cooked his meals in his studio. It was a large open space with a kitchen in one corner and a bed closet for him to sleep in. His wife lived a few streets away on Kuipersstraat in their family home, but he mostly only saw her on the weekends. His two children had grown up and left the city to work in London and Berlin.

He loved his wife, but it was his work, painting, that he felt an urgent need to concentrate on. He hated wasting a minute not thinking about, or working on a painting. With a growing sense of urgency, the painter wanted to complete his life's work while he was still able to.

As usual he awoke at 7 am, made breakfast and brewed his coffee. He wandered down the street to the local Albert Heijn store for food supplies. Then he sat down in front of his canvas and painted.

During the day he often had a break and strolled down Govert Flinckstraat the short distance to the Amstel and sat by the riverbank to watch the canal boats chug past and the cyclists pedal along the river bank.

Most afternoons he took a walk through the old city. Today as he set off there was a warm September breeze rustling through the full grown leaves of the plain trees on Stadhouderskade. The luscious aroma of late summer mixed with sea air and fragrant flowers tinged with the musty, sweet scent of hashish as he passed by the local coffee shop.

He loved the sounds of Amsterdam. The church and clock tower bells chiming throughout the day in singsong slightly off key melodies. The squeal of the trams as they scooted along their rails. The constant tinkle tinkle of bicycle bells as they gracefully glided along the streets in an almost constant stream.

He wandered into the Gracths crossing Singlegracht and continued into Centrum. He zigzagged along the canals crossing one bridge then walked left until he came to the next bridge, crossed that bridge and turned left again. After Single he crossed Lijnbaangracht, then Prinsen, Keizers and Herengrachts.

Now tired, he rested on a bench on Brouwersgracht and watched the world go by. The world really did go by. People from everywhere walked, cycled or floated by in canal cruisers with the tour guide describing the scene in Korean, Chinese or Italian.

Watching cyclists was his favourite pastime. People of all ages and dress cycled to and from work, the shops, bars and everywhere. Men in suits with their phones pressed to their ears. Mothers with babies in the cargo holds of their 'Bakfiets'. Women of all ages some dressed for the office or an evening out in high heels and revealing skirts. Casual young women, their hair flowing and bare legs in mini skirts or shorts pumped their pedals with such confidence and strength. The dynamism of the girls riding past him, rosy cheeks and serene expressions, the combination of movement and feminine beauty stirred him. To the painter these were the most beautiful sights in elegant, old, picturesque and lovely Amsterdam.

When he attended art school and for many years after, he went to figure drawing and painting sittings. But now he didn't need them, he just watched the cyclists and people going about their daily lives and that gave him everything he needed for his paintings.

After several minutes resting he continued on his way meandering back along the canals. Crossing Keizersgracht and turning into Nieuwe Spiegelstraat, he stopped to look in the window of Kramer Antiek. This shop had a large collection of Delft ceramics and other interesting antiques for sale. He always had a look as he went past to see if there was anything new that he might be tempted to add to his collection.

He soon reached the end of Spiegelstraat and crossed Singlegracht to the front of the Rijksmuseum. He walked around the grand 19th century building to Museumplein, past the Van Gough and Stedelijk museums to Van Baerlestraat and continued to Ceintuurbaan. Soon the road took him into Sarphatipark and out the other end to cross Van Woustraat.

He decided to visit his wife just a few blocks away.

'Hello darling, how has your day been?' he said to Elke.

'I have had a nice day Peter,' she replied. 'On Friday you have the dealers from Antwerp and Brussels visiting during the day and my party in the evening, don't forget.'

'Oh no, another day wasted!' Peter lamented.

'It will not be a waste of time darlink. I hope the dealers will want to take several paintings.'

'Yes, but I will have to talk, and be nice to them and everyone at the party. It takes up so much time and energy.'

'Oh, you'll survive. Then next week I'm going to Paris to see the dealers there. I'll be gone for a week,' she said.

His wife had been looking after his business affairs for many years. When he first gained some fame, he left the business of selling his work to his dealer in London. But when he met Elke a few years later she insisted, 'Peter, you are being undersold and underpaid. You have to take control of your career and business.'

Elke came from a family of art and antique dealers in Holland, so he put her in charge of his affairs. She placed his paintings with several important art dealers across Europe and many for sold for higher prices that he had achieved in London. Fortunately, unlike some artists, he had always been prolific churning out paintings weekly or monthly at worst. Most years he had completed around thirty saleable works and apart from a few dips in output when they had children he had kept up the pace for many years.

Elke had done such a good job of representing him that when she suggested that they move from London to her home town of Amsterdam he agreed without hesitation.

'You will be closer to the European markets, and you will be inspired,' she said.

She was right on both counts. His figure paintings, landscapes and still lifes were more popular in France and Germany than they were in England or the USA. The Europeans liked his more impressionist style. In England they wanted shocking or outlandish abstract art. But his portraits were popular there as at that time he painted personalities from the London arts and film scene.

He felt at home in Amsterdam, as if he was always meant to be there. The only connection to England that still tugged at his heart was the girl he left behind. But it was she that left him, and he had no idea where she was now, or if she was even still alive.

Elke made him a cup of coffee and they chatted for a while.

'I'm going to go back to the studio now and work on my landscape.'

'Have you pulled out the paintings for the dealers to see on Friday?'

'No, I have no idea which paintings they will like my love.'

'Of course you don't, that's my job. I will come over at about 11 on Friday morning and arrange everything. The Van Stoep's will arrive at 12. See you then schatse.'

They kissed goodbye and the painter returned to his studio and worked until late in the evening on his painting.

2

The next morning the painter sat down in front of his easel as he did every day. He held his brush lightly in his hand and swished the clean bristles around in the palm of his free hand. He looked at the blank white canvas in front of him and slowly an image appeared to him, filling in the space until it was bursting with colour and vivid images in his mind. Then he set to work mixing burnt umber colour with linseed oil in perpetration to apply his first dark colour.

The door bell chimed, ding dong. He glanced at the clock, 10 am. He had agreed to help a new teacher from the art school. The head of the school had asked if he would meet the man, show him his studio and how he worked. The painter had worked with several of the art school employees over the years. Although he had never been an a teacher himself, he sometimes gave guest lectures. They called him master. He liked the respect the name implied, but he knew he didn't deserve to be called master, like Rembrandt.

He opened the door and saw a tall handsome fellow with dark curly hair and a trimmed beard. He looked young and earnest. 'Hello Gregor,' he said as he stood aside and beckoned the young man to enter.

'Thank you Master for agreeing to see me.'

'Of course, anything for the school. I'm only too happy to impart some of my knowledge, and Professor Van Damme assures me that you are very talented.'

Gregor walked in and looked around the room. Paintings were hung on all four walls from to the top of the high ceilinged studio to near the level of the wooden floor three or four deep. A large set of windows took up half of the space on one wall and looked out onto the communal gardens with many trees and houses on the other side.

A table was placed In the middle of the room covered in jars filled with paint brushes and tubes of oil paint some new, many squeezed to near empty. A tall easel stood next to the table with a large blank canvas held in its grips. In front of it was a stool.

The room smelled of linseed oil and turpentine and the pallid morning light made soft edges and left many dark spaces in the corners of the large open space.

'I see you are about to begin a painting Master, forgive me for intruding.'

'You are not intruding, I was just musing in front of the canvas trying to decide what to paint, and call me Peter, please.'

'So you haven't yet decided what you are going to paint.'

'I never do. Every morning I try to start a new painting. I have many half conceived ideas in my head. Sometime inspiration comes, and sometimes not. If my mind stays blank for too long I go back to one of my many uncompleted projects.'

Gregor slowly walked around the room examining the paintings. There were indeed many works in progress lining the walls with yet more stacked on the floor leaning against the walls. There were still lives with flowers and fruit, pastoral scenes, moody interiors with shadowy figures, abstract splashes of colour, cubist explosions, and nudes, both male and female.

'Peter, you do have a lot of paintings on the go, and so many different styles and subjects.'

'Well Gregor, if you want to paint for a living, to be an artist, you have to be proficient in all styles of painting. Today you may say, 'I will paint a Rembrandt portrait', the next, an early Picasso. No matter what the style or subject you must be able to accomplish it.

'However, eventually, you must confront the real problem that every would-be artist faces, their existential crisis, what do *I* want to paint? What do *I* have to say?'

'What is it that you want to paint Peter?'

'Life,' he answered. 'A life, all of life, life from beginning to end. I want to transcend time and paint the whole sum of a person. I want the viewer to see every experience that the subject endured and let their true nature shine out through it all. One year or one thousand years, every sigh and blow, every emotion and experience. So that the viewer can see the entire story and understand, touch the true nature of my subject which could be a cup, an apple or a person.'

'You have succeeded many times over. Your prolific work is world famous.'

'No no, I have failed miserably. I have never succeeded in achieving that. This failure tears at my heart. I long for success. But now, I am old, and I fear I will never reach my goal.'

'You aren't that old. Have heart and never give in. But you must have come close at least?'

'Once I did, an old subject. It was a painting of a woman, a girl. But the painting is lost. It pains me too much to even remember it.'

'It is a shame that you no longer have the painting. But now time has passed and you are a more complete artist. Perhaps you can recreate it and finally achieve your goal.'

'It's not so simple Gregor. I have to have the vision, feel the passion. What I had, I lost. It was my own fault of course. No, I don't think I can ever get back that feeling of completeness. The sense of oneness with my subject, the girl I loved.'

'So she was your first love, the one that broke your heart? I can see that the cut was deep. But you are married and your love of your wife is famous.'

'Ah, you come too close. I can't express myself very well in words. This is why I am a painter, my expression is visual. Ignore what I just said, it was mere meanderings.'

The conversation awakened his memory, and now after many years of hiding it away in the deepest recesses of his heart, the door creaked open and the memory of her musky scent awakened his senses. His mind was now filled with her movements, her laugh, glinting eyes and luscious hair. He felt as if he could touch her after crossing an ocean of time. His first love filled his vision. But now, as then, all those years ago, the vision faded, she was gone and he was alone once more.

Gregor asked, 'You don't do many portraits nowadays do you? There are many famous portraits in your early work.'

'No I haven't painted portraits for years.'

'What about figure paintings, nudes?

'No, I no longer do figure painting either.'

'So you don't use models any longer?

'No, Gregor, as I said, I want to paint the essence of my subjects. To do that for a real live person is emotionally and physically draining. I need to feel so much empathy with the sitter I must become them. No, it is too difficult for me now.

'Instead I paint from my memory, my imagination. That way I only have to take on the persona of the image in my mind, not a real living and breathing creature. Just a two dimensional image. So if I paint a woman, she can be dancing, or gazing, or loving. But she is not alive. When I put the brush down, I can leave her on the canvas. With a live sitter the character haunts me day and night.'

'Maybe if you found the right sitter you could finish the masterpiece you long to create.'

'No no, Gregor, now I only want to paint the visions that come to me from everyday life. The scenes I see played out around me here in Amsterdam. But all this talk of art has exhausted me. I must rest now, please leave.'

'I will leave you now of course, but may I return?'

'Yes yes come another day.'

'I have a friend I would like to bring along. She would love to see your studio.'

'Yes Gregor, bring her along why not,' he said ushering him out the door.

He sat in front of his blank canvas again. The vision he had glimpsed of his new work had vanished from his mind's eye. He sat for as long as he could bear then gave up. 'Ah, it's gone, my day is ruined!'

He decided to go for a walk instead. He slammed the door to his studio and creaked down the narrow and steep staircase and opened the front door. He squeezed past rows of parked bicycles and walked down Govert Flinckstraat, through Albert Cuypmarkt to Sarphati Park to feed the ducks on the pond.

He sat on a bench and threw crumbs in the water. Swallows flew aerobatics over the pond chasing insects. He picked out one swallow and locked his eyes onto it following it as it flew up then banked hard left swooping around in a graceful arc and pulling up to a stall to catch an insect then plunging down again to pick up speed pulling straight just above the water of the pond and whirling around to the right.

He loved to watch birds, and he could paint them in any pose, resting or flying. He had it all captured in his head.

His meeting with Gregor had disturbed him. It had awakened his memory of the lost painting of his lost lover. He had nearly captured her essence in the painting and was close to completing it. But then there was that night, and she was gone. When he finally accepted that she was never going to return to him, he destroyed the painting in tears and torment, but that was so many years ago.

After a while he grew weary of watching the birds and returned to the studio. He worked on his paintings as best as he could for the rest of the week. After a few days he managed to drive Gregor and his lost masterpiece from his mind.

3

On Friday morning the painter's wife breezed into the studio. She was wearing a kaftan and a long silk scarf that wafted out behind her as she strode into the studio.

'Goedemorgen schatse, have you finished any more paintings?' she asked.

'No Elke, just more ideas and half finished works.'

'Well no problem, I will pull out a selection for the dealers.'

She rummagged through the paintings stacked on the ground and separated out out paintings that she thought would sell.

'Ah, this one yes. Oh schatse, I had forgotten abou this one! Why has this not bee sold before now? It will walk out the door. This one, no. I think I will take this away and put it in a cupboard somewhere, it's awful.'

'What do you mean Elke? I love that painting, leave it be.'

'Oh no, Peter, it should be hidden away. You can put it in your bed closet if you like. But this one, yes, this was completed this year. I will put it on the easel and it can be the showpiece for our salon today.'

She picked up the large painting of a street scene of Amsterdam. There were trees along a canal and elegant waterfront buildings with cyclists moving back and forth. Birds flew through the air and Van Gough like clouds filled the sky.

'Yes darlink, this painting will sell to the boys from Antwerp for sure. Now let me see. What else have we got. This one, yes, how exciting!'

'No Elke, not that one, I can never sell that one, give it to me!'

Peter grabbed the painting from Elke, but she refused to let go of it. They wrestled with the painting bending the frame and pushing their elbows and foreheads into the canvas.

'Stop schatse, you're damaging the painting.'

Finally Elke managed to wrest the painting from Peter who slumped into a chair.

'It's not finished in any case,' he said.

Elke put it against the wall and stood back to regard it.

'Of course it's finished. If it wasn't for me you would never say a painting is finished. You would continue working on them for ever and a day.'

'You're right darling, none of my painting are up to scratch,' said Peter shaking his head in despair.

'Schatse, don't be sad.'

Elke crouched down and cupped the painter's face in her hands and kissed him on the forehead.

'Come now, your work is wonderful, people are moved by your paintings. More importantly your paintings move out the door. They sell fast. What better confirmation of your worth and talent could there be? Cheer up my dear, the Belgians will be here soon.'

She continued rummaging and looking at the paintings that were hung on the wall. She placed the paintings she had chosen strategically around the studio. Turning her attention to the state of the room she tidied things away, hiding sweaters and socks under the cushions on the sofa. She opened the windows to let some air in and washed his dishes and coffee cups that were placed empty and stained all around the studio.

Finally satisfied, she sat down on the sofa and took out a handkerchief to wipe her brow.

'Oh I'm exhausted now,' she proclaimed. 'I had better go and make myself beautiful.'

She went to the bathroom to touch up her make up and comb her hair. She re-emerged with a beaming smile on her face and threw her scarf over her shoulder dramatically.

'Now I'm ready to receive our guests.'

She looked ruefully at her husband. 'Go change your clothes. You look like a rag-a-muffin.'

Peter dutifully went to his bed closet and opened the big drawer below the bed and puled out a clean shirt and trousers. He changed his shoes, putting on an elegant pair of two toned loafers. He put a red cravat around his neck and tied a knot that he pushed to one side. He took his beret off the hatstand by the door and looking in the mirror placed it on his head, cocked it to one side and pulled it down.

'There, how's that?'

'You look so handsome darlink, oh, as beautiful as the day we met.'

The doorbell chimed, ding dong and Elke went to open the door. Speaking in Dutch she ushered two thin men dressed in black suits and wearing horn rimmed glasses into the studio.

'Peter, you remember the Van Der Stoep brothers, Baaf and Edgardo,' she said smiling while waving her hands in a flourish.

'Yes, yes of course I remember Baaf and Edgardo. How are you both? You look so well.'

The identical twins bowed their heads in unison. One of them, Peter felt sure it was Baaf, started speaking in a dialect that Peter could not understand at all. Baaf nodded his head towards Edgardo who took up where Baaf left off. Peter, totally confused, smiled and nodded his head enthusiastically.

Elke put her arm around Baaf's shoulder and whispering to him in Dutch guided him and Edgardo towards the paintings she had put on display. She pointed to one and stood back as if in awe at the beauty of the work.

The two men from Antwerp rubbed their thin boney chins and murmured to each other. They nodded to indicate that they had concluded their deliberations and continued to the next painting.

Elke walked them around the room and they spent several minutes examining each of the works. Fianally she brought them to the showcase painting on the easel.

The brothers stood back and rubbed their chins for an exceptionally long time. Eventually, Edgardo looked at Peter.

'Master, do you still paint portraits?' he asked in English.

'Portraits? No, I haven't painted a portrait for many years. Why are you interested in portraits now?'

'Baaf raised his finger to show that he would be the one to respond. There is a renewed interest in portraits. We are always asked about them but so few artists are painting them. Your portraits are wonderful, they have been your finest work over the years. They still trade for the highest prices of any of your works. Indeed Peter, if it wasn't for your fame as a portrait artist your other works would attract lower prices.'

Edgardo continued, 'I think telephones are the reason people want portraits.'

'Telephones?' said Elke puzzled.

'Yes Elke, telephones,' said Baaf.

'I think it is the new cultural importance of the selfie that has gripped the artistic subconciousness,' said Edgardo.

Baaf continued, 'Everyone is taking selfies. They think that this is art, and when they come into our gallery they are surprised there are so few smiling faces beaming out at them from the canvaces. That after all, is what they see all around them in normal life.'

'Slefies? You must be insane. I am an artist, I don't do happy snaps for imbecile tourists! How about cats? Would you like me to paint cats also?'

In unison Baaf and Edgardo smilled, raised their index fingers, nodded enthusiastically and said, 'Cats! Yes please, we can sell as many pictures of cats as you can supply us.'

A short while later, after Elke had shown the brothers from Antwerp out the door, the painter and his wife slumped down into the sofa.

'Schatse, I'm sorry. The brothers have sold so many of your painting in the past. I had no idea they were going so down market now. They say the market has changed, and they need to find new types of material to sell.'

'Never mind my darling, as long as you don't want me to start painting selfies,' said Peter.

'Although they are right of course. Your most famous paintings are your portraits. But no matter, in a few minutes Monsieur Dupont from Brussels will be arriving. We shall see what's in fashion for paintings in the Belgian capital. He sells mostly to EU diplomats and politicians. A totally different market.'

The painter and his wife had moved from London to Amsterdam thirty years ago. But Peter had struggled to learn Dutch. Part of the problem was that Dutch people invariably spoke better English than he could ever hope to speak Dutch. So they usually replied to his falting destruction of their language in English, and the conversation continued that way.

The other problem was that people from different regions in Holland and Flemish Belgium spoke different dialects. They did not just sound different but used different words and idioms. Dutch people could move between the dialects without difficulty. But outsiders were soon left behind.

A short while later the doorbell rang again and Elke showed French speaking Marcel Dupont into the studio.

'Hello Marcel, so nice to see you again,' said Peter.

'Always a pleasure to see what you have been working on my dear Peter,' said Marcel smiling and shaking Peter's hand.

'Come, let me show you his latest oeuvre,' said Elke. She took Marcel directly to the showcase painting on the easel.

'I love it,' he said. 'Of course I must have this one. It will quickly sell I am sure.'

'So you don't want me to do portraits?' Asked Peter.

'If you would like to come to Brussels and paint EU bureaucrats and politicians I am sure you could make a market. But the people I sell to aren't interested in anybody else's image. They only want to see themselves, on TV, the internet. Or they want their illustrious portrait added to a staircase or conference room somewhere in the EU buildings.

'But this painting of Amsterdam will be popular. They can take it back to their offices in Poland or Slovenia and they will seem like cultured world travellers.'

Marcel said he would take the Amsterdam scene and four other paintings on consignment. After pleasantries he got up to leave. Muoi, muoi, Elke kissed him on both cheeks, 'So nice to see you Marcel. The paintings will be ready for shipment as soon as possible.'

Pleased with their days work, Elke and Peter hugged as they said goodbye. 'You won't forget to come to my soirée?' asked Elke.

'No, of course not darling, I'll see you this evening,' said Peter.

After their children had grown up and left home, the two of them had agreed that Peter would live in the studio and Elke would stay in their family home. Elke liked to entertain, staging elaborate parties. During the day her friends would drop by the apartment and have a chat while drinking coffee and eating cake. She was involved in several charities and was on the councils of several art institutions across Holland.

Peter had become more reclusive and shied away from all the noise and people that Elke loved. He began to spend some nights sleeping at the studio, and eventually moved in full time.

This evening she had arranged an informal drinks and canapés affair. He had no idea who would be there and cared not. But he would go along for a while to keep his wife happy

Now he was alone again and he placed his blank canvas back on the easel.

4

As the twilight light changed to a dreamy summer mood the painter put down his paint brush and changed his clothes for his wife's soirée. He put on his red cravat and pulled his beret over to the left, just so. I must get into character, he thought.

He climbed the narrow stairs to the top floor apartment. The door was open and as he approached he heard laughter and glasses clinking.

Elke was in the far corner of the living room talking to a group of people, waving her arms in the air in a dramatic way. She was wearing a gold coloured kaftan and turban. The apartment was filled with people.

Peter went into his old study to escape the crowd, but there were several people in there already. He was about to leave when Professor Van Damme said, 'Dear Peter how are you,' his beaming face close to his.

'Van Damme, sorry I didn't see you there, I'm fine thanks. I met that fellow from the school you wanted me to see, Gregor.'

'Yes, you did indeed and he is here tonight, let me see, oh there he is, come and say hello.'

Van Damme lead Peter back into the living room to where Gregor was standing by a window.

'Peter, good to see you again.' said Gregor. 'Let me introduce you to my fiance, Elenore.'

A graceful young woman standing next to Gregor raised her hand for him to shake. Peter instinctively took it gently and kissed the back of her fingers.

'Delighted to meet you Elenore.'

She smiled and bowed her head slightly. Peter was struck by her smile and eyes. She looked so reminiscent, so much like the women he knew in his youth. She was full of life, charm, relaxed and confident.

'So Peter this is your family home?' said Gregor.

'Yes it is, but I spend most of my time at the studio nowadays.'

Van Damme and Gregor peppered Peter with questions about his life in Amsterdam and his children. They wanted to know more about his recent work. Peter answered as matter of factly as he could. He disliked chit chat. All the while he could not stop glancing at Elenore, her large brown eyes, full lips and elegant neck.

Van Damme and Gregor discussed the work in the student exhibition that was to be held soon. Peter nodded, but their voices merged into the noise of the party.

'Tell me Elenore, what to you do?' he said.

'I work at the Rijksmuseum in administration.'

'Are you an artist Elenore?' Peter asked.

'I draw a little,' she said.

'She does some life modelling at the school, people draw her,' Gregor piped in.

Peter looked up at Gregor and Van Damme. They had stopped talking, noticing the Peter was no longer listening to them.

'Gregor told me about your studio. I would love to see it sometime,' said Elenore.

Peter turned back to her, 'Why not this evening? It's only around the corner,' he said.

'Ah, thanks for the invite,' said Gregor, 'let's enjoy the party first.'

Van Damme raised his hand and said, 'Look, there is the Director of the Stedelijk, let me introduce these two to him.'

Peter nodded politely as Van Damme lead them away, weaving their way though the crowd to the other side of the room.

Peter squeezed between people talking and clinking their glasses until he was standing next to his wife.

Elke welcomed him into the centre of a circle of admiring people. Peter was the star attraction, as he always was at Elke's parties. She showed him off and he smiled politely.

Elke takes care of business, thank goodness, so I don't have to. All I have to do is play the master painter every now and then, he reminded himself.

'Oh darlink, you look so handsome. Let me introduce you to Louis who is a curator at the National Gallery in London.'

'Charmed to meet you Peter, I am a great admirer of your work. I hope we will see some new figure paintings from you soon,' said a smiling man bowing as he put out his hand for Peter to shake.

'Peter you remember Maestro Rodrigo from the Giovine Orchestra Genoa,' said Elke.

On it went, his evening on the red carpet, playing royalty to the upper echelons of the European art industry. At least the ones who happened to be in Amsterdam that week for what ever reason. None of them would miss Elke's soirée, unless there was something better on. But Elke was too canny to allow that to happen. Her parties were always perfectly timed so as not to clash with any other evening event, and she only held them when there was something happening in Amsterdam that would attract the right people.

The circle of people around Elke and Peter continually changed as guests were introduced to Peter, made a few sentences of polite conversation, until the circle turned once more, and the next person was introduced.

Peter was talking to the director of a Swiss museum when he noticed Elenore across the room. She was with Gregor who was holding forth talking insistently to some fellow. Elenore was pretending to be involved and interested. But Peter noticed, yes, she is, she's looking at me. He smiled at the Swiss gentleman and nodded, but he could not avert his eyes from Elenore.

The circle turned, and he was now introduced to a large woman with an even larger hat. She was, 'Sooo delighted to meet the great master,' she said in an exaggerated posh English accent.

Peter looked again towards Elenore and she was looking straight at him. I am the centre of attention, of course she's looking at me. Nothing more to read into that, he thought. But he felt an attraction to her that he had not felt towards any woman for as long as he could remember.

He turned his back to Elenore, and the circle of people, including Elke, shuffled their feet and rearranged the circle to a new orientation around the painter.

Peter endured as long as he could. Eventually, he caught Elke's eye, and she understood. 'Oh darlink, you have been so gracious this evening. You can go whenever is suits you dear. I'll come over and see you before I leave for Paris,' she whispered into his ear.

Peter waited for Elke to start speaking in a loud voice to the circle of people in general about some topic of the day. That was his queue that he could shuffle away while the audience was distracted.

As he reached the front hallway on his way out he passed Elenore and Gregor who was talking with great passion to some poor man whose bored eyes were transfixed on Gregor's convulsed face.

'Peter, are you leaving?' said Elenore, touching his elbow.

'Yes, parties are not for me.'

'What about the tour of your studio?'

'Come over in a little while if you like. Don't leave it too late.'

'I would like to. I will drag Gregor away soon if I can.'

As he walked down Van Woustraat Peter took off his beret and cravat and stuffed them in his pocket. He soon arrived at the studio, and after only a short while the doorbell chimed.

He opened the door, 'Come in, you are both welcome,' he said.

'Thank you Peter, may we look around?' said Gregor.

'Yes of course.'

The couple paced along the walls of the studio regarding the many artworks.

'This is a very interesting work,' said Gregor pointing to a pastel drawing of a female nude high up on the wall.'

'That was just an exercise, a study that I did some years ago.'

'Do you still paint from live models? Asked Elenore'

'No, not for years. I have no time or need for models any longer. I paint from the visions I have in my head.'

Elenore smiled at him and continued to stroll along the row of paintings. She was not tall but slender. Her face was a perfect shape for her well proportioned body.

'I've seen many photos of your paintings,' said Elenore.

Gregor said, 'She was interested to see some of your work up close, and your studio. She was impressed that I had met you.'

'Well I hope you enjoy my works. The best ones aren't in the studio of course. They've been sold. Still there are a few on display here that I am happy with,' said Peter.

'They are very good,' said Elenore. 'I like your city scenes, but there are no portraits here.'

'Why does everyone go on about my portraits? I have told everyone, I do not do portraits anymore.'

'Your figure paintings are my favourites, though,' she said.

'Peter, maybe it's time that you painted from life again, so you can complete your work, recreate your masterpiece,' said Gregor.

Peter was puzzled by this intrusion, people pushing him to paint portraits and nudes that he didn't want to paint anymore. 'Did Professor Van Damme put you up to this?' demanded Peter.

'No, not at all Peter. Rather, when I found out that you were connected to the school and the Professor said I could meet you, it was your figure paintings that I thought of. Then you told me that you had never completed your masterpiece. I, we, would like to help you. That is all, just some encouragement from admirers.'

Until Peter had met Elenore he was sure that he would never use a model again. But he now looked at her in a new light. She had bright shining eyes. Her face was beautiful. But he could not see her figure under her loose clothes.

'You say you would like to help me?'

'Yes, if we can,' said Gregor.

'Elenore does life modelling? She could sit for me. Perhaps that will encourage me to try once more,' said Peter

Elenore's eyes drooped to the floor and she swished around and walked back up the line of paintings. She looked at Gregor. He smiled back at her. 'I don't mind chéri. Why not?' he said.

Elenore turned to look at the painter, 'I'll do it, if you're sure you want me to,' she said.

'I think so, but show me,' said Peter, 'I need to see what you look like.'

Elenore's face retreated, she looked taken aback. 'What, right now?'

'Yes yes, let's have a look. I have no time to waste my dear.'

She looked around the room for some where to disrobe.

'Over there,' Peter pointed to Chinese blinds in a corner of the studio. They had been used by his models in the past.

Elenore went behind them and one by one her garments were draped over the divider. Soon she emerged, naked, and stood in the middle of the room. She did several quick poses, as models do at the start of a life drawing class. Then she stopped and stood silently before Peter.

Her body was beautiful. She had a perfect figure with a thin waist with well proportioned behind and thighs. Her breasts were firm but soft and welcoming.

'Please, turn around.' he said.

She slowly turned a full circle with her arms outstretched.

'Alright, I will paint you. I would like to start as soon as possible, when can you come?'

'It depends, how many sittings do you think you will need?' asked Elenore.

'As many as it takes. I told Gregor, I don't paint in half measures. It is all or nothing for me. I will continue until I finish. I will pay the standard modelling fee of course.'

Elenore put her clothes back on and stood whispering to Gregor. After a few minutes Gregor said, 'She will come tomorrow if you like.'

'Tomorrow it is at 10 am, sharp,' said Peter.

He showed them out giving nothing more of his emotions away. They seemed a little unsure of themselves as they departed. Peter hadn't though they would agree so easily. But it was all Gregor's fault, his suggestion.

Peter had early success painting celebrity portraits. That's why they think my portraits are the best. It is because the sitters are famous, not because the paintings are good, he thought.

Sevdral of his portraits had been purchased by museums, and they brought him fame. But they were not his best paintings at all, in his opinion. I painted some famous people. Big deal, the paintings are in museums, ridiculous.

Far from considering them, '*his most important contributions to contemporary art*', as one famous Australian art critic described them, he thought they were actually terrible.

He considered some of his life paintings, nudes, to be very good and they also sold well. He was happy about their success.

Some people have taste, understand the meaning of human expression, he mused.

In his mind, the best work he ever created was of his lover Lana whom he painted at the beginning of his career, soon after graduating from Goldsmiths College, so long ago.

Ah, Lana, what a beautiful girl, what memories, what a painting. It was the closest I have ever come to creating a painting that lived by itself, something alive and real, he lamented.

Peter was interested in depicting the human condition as vulnerable, tender, transcendent and sublime. He had no wish to paint heroes, or fallen angels, but living humans, true to their inherent nature.

But after Lana left him that night, no, he could never get back to that paradise lost. He flet abandoned, in a struggle for survival, searching for meaning. He was lost in a confusion of broken images and pain, until he met Elke. She consoled him, and brought him understand that life is to be lived. 'Heaven can wait, at least a little while,' she said.

But now, yes, he could see in Elenore the elements he needed to make his perfect painting, the essence of his lover. He felt he could achieve the same completeness that he had accomplished with his original work.

There was something about her erotic persona that stirred him the same way as Lana. She had the same fire in her eyes. He was intrigued by her. The painter determined to try once more, to strive for perfection. He was now filled with excitement and could barley wait to embark on his new project.

5

Peter slept lightly that night he was so excited. He woke early as usual and made his breakfast.

He then prepared a few props around the studio for his model to use. His models stand had been neglected for a long time and was in a corner with a bookshelf on it. He pulled it to the centre of the room and dusted it off. He Dragged the sofa to the side of the stand at an angle to the windows so as to catch the morning light and arranged chairs in various positions.

Rummaging in his art supply cabinet he pulled out one large and one small drawing pad. He made sure he had a good supply of charcoals, pastels and a sheaf of loose paper ready on his table.

Waiting for what seemed like eternity, at 10 am sharp, ding dong, the doorbell chimed and he rushed to the door.

'Good morning Elenore, please come in.'

Elenore's eyes fixed on his, with a faint smile she proceeded without talking to the Chinese blinds and disrobed.

The painter waved his hand at towards the stand and she took her place.

'I would like you to make a series of gestures and then hold the pose for one minute please,' he said.

She stretched her arms out forward as in a ballet move and bent her knees in a soft plié.

After a minute the painter said, 'New pose.'

She hesitated, then moved. This time she put her hands on her hips and twisted her torso to the right keeping her legs firm and straight.

Peter sat on his stool and drew her gestures on his small pad, quickly with a square piece of charcoal. Morning light streamed diagonally through the windows illuminating her body highlighting her contours and her shape. He only made quick outlines of her as if feeling out the limits of her body, it's size and proportions.

After ten poses, he said, 'You can rest now.'

Without speaking she returned to the Chinese blinds and put on a robe that she had brought with her.

'Would you like some fruit?' said Peter gesturing towards a bowl in the kitchen.'

'Yes thank you,' said Elenore picking up an apple.

She took a bite and walked to the sofa and sat down. After a few minutes, Peter said, 'New pose, this time five minutes.'

Elenore unwrapped her robe, leaving it behind her on the sofa and resumed her position on the stand. She made a new gesture, still standing.

Peter continued to draw with his charcoal this time making thicker smudged lines, feeling out her form and weight.

'New pose, but sit now. You won't be able to hold many poses for five minutes if you are standing. Do something different,' said Peter.

She sat down, and her gestures became more exaggerated. She folded her body over like Rodin's La Danaid. The next pose she arched backwards, her arms outstretched and hands propped on the sofa supporting her weight with her breasts thrust upwards.

Peter drew her, searching for her inner impulse, the motivation that precipitated each gesture that ended in the pose that resulted.

She held six poses, then once again, Peter said, 'You may rest now.'

She put on her robe, laid back on the sofa and closed her eyes.

'Very good Elenore, you are an excellent model. Take ten minutes to rest.'

'Thank you master,' said Elenore.

'Master?' Peter chuckled. 'You are not my servant. I am your servant, your admirer.'

Peter put his small pad down and cast his fingers across his box of pastels rolling them as if along piano keys. He chose one and placed it on his large drawing pad in preparation.

After a while Elenore opened her eyes and glanced a the clock on the wall. Ten minutes had passed and shes asked, 'Do you wish a longer pose this time?'

'Yes, stay where you are on the sofa.'

She slipped off her robe and lying on her side curled up her legs and rested her head on her hand with her elbow on the sofa and yawned.

Peter moved his stool in front of the window to see her with the light shining directly on her and began to draw.

He drew shapes, the lines of arms, legs, the curve of her muscles and belly. He wasn't interested in her, the woman, only in capturing her form. But he knew this would soon change. To make an interesting painting he needed more than an elegant or beautiful gesture or body. He needed the seek out the uniqueness of his model, her inner self.

At least this was his idea, his desire. Other figure painters had different approaches. He had studied the greats of course at college and all his life, Leonardo, Rembrandt.

'Picasso, the greatest portraitist of all time,' he mumbled to himself.

'What was that about Picasso Peter?'

'I was just saying to my self, he was able to capture something immortal, the essence of humanity. Picasso didn't use models, at least not after his younger years. He painted and drew from his memory. But he knew the people he was depicting. He would always be drawing while he was talking, eating, drinking. He observed everyone, their gestures, the way they moved. He spent much time with the people he depicted, the women in his life, especially his lovers, his wives.'

'So are you are going to paint me with three heads and bulging eyes?' Asked Elenore.

'No, it was Picasso's early portraits that I am referring to.

'You said that you hadn't used models for a long time. Why do you want me now?'

'Because Gregor, Van Damme, yourself, everyone seems to want me to paint a real person again. I have tried before to achieve some perfection, but I failed. This time, with you, perhaps I will succeed.

'Other artists use a model for a few sessions to obtain what they need. For a long time I have preferred to paint only from memory and reference drawings I have made. But I see now that those works have been lifeless. My landscapes and still lives have been popular because they seem genuine to the viewers. But my paintings of people have, at least in my mind, missed the mark, failures, which is why I gave up. With you I feel I have another chance to succeed, to paint a human being again.'

'How many sessions will you need me for?'

'I don't know Elenore. This painting is different. I am trying to go back to what I had once achieved, or nearly. I want to capture you, on canvas that is.'

Elenore felt sleepy, relaxed. She had been trepidatious about modelling for the painter. Gregor had encouraged her, 'He's a famous painter, it will do you good, give you notoriety to be his muse,' he said.

I don't need notoriety, she thought, but she was intrigued by Peter. Now having agreed to come and pose for him, she felt as if it was natural. She felt shielded and happy under his gaze.

Then the painter said, 'New pose.'

She glanced at the clock, and 15 minutes had elapsed. She sat up put her feet on the floor and stretched her arms.

Peter said, 'I want something different this time. Here, allow me.' He gently put his hand on her ankle and lifted her leg up and onto the sofa and raising her knee, 'Lie backwards,' he said.

She stretched back with her head on a cushion and went to lift her other leg onto the sofa but Peter said, 'No, leave your foot where it is.'

He placed a chair straight in front of her and sat down, looking at her prone body with her legs spread. He picked up his pad and began to draw.

For the first time Elenore felt uneasy, compromised.

'Don't worry Elenore. I am just trying a pose. I don't know if it will be what ultimately reveals you to me, but I must look at you in every way.' Peter smiled, 'I'm not so interested in your anatomy. I want to free you from your inhibitions. I must know you intimately. There can be no holding back.'

He drew fast making scraping sounds with the pastel. After some time he said, 'New pose, please turn sideways.'

He stood up and touched her ankle, gently he hooked her leg over the arm of the sofa, picked up her hands and folded them across her belly.

Continuing to draw quickly, his eyes never seemed to leave her to check what he had drawn. He had a slight smile on his face, but seemed lost in concentration.

Peter continued to talk to her while he drew. 'You are right about Picasso of course. At the beginning of the 20th century, our conceptions of art were thrown up in the air. When they landed, we had Fauvism,

Expressionism, Cubism, Dada and Surrealism. Artists painted people from their dreams, subconscious and divorced them entirely from what they actually looked like.

'I'm not interested in the surrealist dream image, stylised or exploded. But the true nature of the model, what ever that might be, and I have to find that out about you.'

After this pose Peter looked at the clock and said, 'Time's up, that's it for today.'

It was 12 noon and Elenore put on her clothes.

The next day at 10 am Elenore arrived again at the studio. She disrobed and stood feet apart her arms by her side on the stand. 'What would you like today?'

Peter looked at her and swished a paint brush around in his hand. His eyes followed the contours of her face and ear. He looked at every detail as his eyes continued down her gentle neck to her clavicle, down her arm, breasts and abdomen to her pelvic region and pubis.

Peter knew that to make his painting special, a masterpiece, he needed to come so close to his model, Elenore, that he was inside her skin, and therein was the peril for them both.

'I need more from you. Yesterday you were flat, emotionless. I need to see some tension, something defiant expressive. I know what your body looks like. I can see how you move, your proportions. You are graceful, but now I need something more dynamic.'

Elenore was puzzled. She had posed for drawing classes at the art school many times. She was used to eyes regarding her, seeing her body. But the students were all lifeless. They never spoke or asked anything of her. She just made a gesture and held a pose.

She stepped off the stand and walked around the room, looking at the paintings on the walls. She raised her arms and swung around. She danced around the room turning in circles, while Peter looked at her, his eyes, squinting, critical.

Then she stopped and looked him in the eyes. He stood up and went to her and ran his hands across the skin of her arms and shoulders and back. Dropping to his knees, his hands pressed across her belly and down her behind, squeezing her muscles, caressing her thighs as if feeling a sculpture. He breathed in her scent as his face came close to her body. His lips gently kissed the back of her knee. 'Yes, I need to feel you, drink you in, not just with my eyes, but with all my senses.'

He stood back and went to hes easel. He had pinned a sheet of paper to a large board. Picking up a compressed charcoal stick he began to draw. Soon he pulled the sheet off the easel and replaced it with another.

'New pose, do something more expressive, let me inside of you.'

Elenore tried several poses, each more tormented. Peter drew for several minutes then said 'new pose,' and she tried once more.

This time she lay back on the sofa, leaning on one elbow, her legs apart draped over the edge, her pelvis twisted and sex exposed.

'I like this one,' said Peter

She felt the caress of his eyes, and her skin tingled. She looked at his thin figure, bony hands that seemed so delft, skilled. His movements were quick, his hand moving over the paper and the charcoal making scratching noises. His eyes were fixed on her. She could still feel his hands on her, gentle but insistent.

She smiled, and Peter said, 'What are yo looking so happy about?'

A little laugh came out of her and she covered her mouth with her hand. 'I don't know, I'm relaxing I suppose.'

Peter put his charcoal down and said, 'Yes well, you can relax now. That will do for today.'

'Oh so soon.' Elenore looked at the clock, it was 12 noon. She felt a slight disappointment that the session was over, and she hesitated while putting her clothes back on.

'Would you like a coffee?' asked Peter.

'Yes, thanks.'

Peter made a jug of filter coffee, and they sat down at the kitchen counter together.

'Tell me about Gregor,' said Peter.

'Oh, well, he's my lover, my fiance. We live together.'

'When will you be married?'

'There is no date set yet. He wants to secure his career before making the final commitment.'

'So you are only slightly engaged?' said Peter.

Elenore blushed and looked the painter in the eyes. 'Yes, just a little bit.'

As she was leaving, he went with her to the door. He put his hand over her shoulder to reach the handle. She turned around and looked up into his face her lips parted, her eyes sought out his. They kissed, softly.

'You are so beautiful my dear,' he said.

'Peter, I don't know, but you make me feel special.' She said turning back to the closed door.

Peter turned the handle and pulled the door open. She glanced back at him, her eyes flashing. Then ran down the stairs.

As she walked home her heart pulsed and she felt a flush in her cheeks. Inwardly smiling, fondness for the painter filled her thoughts, like a young girl's crush. He's an eccentric old man, don't get carried away, she told herself.

At the end of the day Gregor came home from work. 'How did the session go today?' he asked.

'It went much better Gregor. I can see that Peter has an artistic idea in mind, and he seems to like the way it's going. He has a nice smile and soft hands.'

'Soft hands? Did he touch you?'

'Yes, he said he needed to experience my form with all his senses, not just sight. He needs to truly understand my physique and get beneath my skin.'

'Elenore, I'm no longer sure this is a good idea! I don't think you should go back again. This is getting out of hand, what have I gotten us into?'

'Gregor, don't be so silly. He just rubbed my shoulders, touched my hands. Besides, he's an old man.'

'Is that all he did? Well, that's perfectly alright then. Standing naked before him and he just rubbed your shoulders. What will he rub next time? Honestly darling I didn't think this through. You should just not go back again. I will go see him and tell him you are too busy for any more sittings.'

'You're a painter yourself, and you even teach life painting. Am I to suppose that you proposition your models?'

'Of course not. I'm a professional, and I don't see the woman, or man for that matter. I'm looking at form, shape, curves. There is nothing erotic about it.'

Elenore folded her arms, looked Gregor in the eye and said, 'It's a different experience being with a real artist, just me and him without a classroom full of students dutifully painting shapes and never moving. He's trying to create something worthwhile, real art. I'm going back tomorrow whether you like it or not. He's a genius, and I want to see the finished work.'

In the early evening Elke left her apartment and walked over to the studio. 'How are you darlink, I came to see you as I'm off to Paris in the morning,' she said as she breezed in the door. 'What a great success my party was, everyone was there.'

Peter was surprised by her visit, and he closed his drawing pad and moved to hide his papers.

Elke looked around the studio and saw the models stand, the easel with a nude drawing on it, and the robe still draped over the Chinese blinds.

'You have a model, no, I don't believe it,' she said. 'Yes, I am going to try again, try to finish my painting.'

'Who is the model, where did you find her?'

'She's from the school, shes the lover of one of the teachers. It's your fault. I met her at your party.'

'Schatse, you don't want to go down this route. You know how sensitive you are. You're playing with fire,' she said.

'No Elke, I will be fine. It's just a painting. Everyone wants me to paint people again.'

'It's just a painting? It's never just a painting for you. Your works are like your children. You love them and never want to let them go. You try do dominate them, own them as if you could live your life in them. Now you want to paint a beautiful young woman? My God, you'll loose yourself Peter.'

'You didn't object to me painting nudes in the past. We made an agreement. I am the painter, and I have full creative control of my work. You are my manager.'

'That was years ago when you were in your prime. You're frail now, emotionally. I don't know where you'll end up. Besides, I leave for Paris tomorrow. You'll be all alone.'

'I forgot that you were going to Paris. When you're there you can sound the dealers out. Do they also wish I would return to figure painting?'

'Alright then, painter, master. I'll go to Paris for a week and sell your paintings for you. I hope you'll still be here when I get back and not have run away with your young model.'

After Elke left, he opened a bottle of wine for the first time in many months. The dry sparkling liquid bubbled down into his stomach and a happiness came over him. Yes, he could see her again, feel her in his heart. It was as if they had just met for the first time.

6

When Peter woke the next morning, his mood had changed. Last night he had fallen asleep with happy memories of Lana and how much she loved him. But now he remembered their separateness, the times when she was cold and uncaring. She would push him away, and he would be in turmoil until she relented and was tender to him once more. He felt betrayed by her. How could she treat him so when he loved her so much?

He tried to put these memories out of his mind and prepared the studio for Elenore. But he knew he needed some tension between him and his model. He could not simply paint a pretty picture and hope to create a masterpiece. He opened the door and waited for Elenore's arrival.

Elenore ran up the stairs, and went straight in.

'You seem happy today,' said Peter.

'I am enjoying our sessions. Would you like the same pose as yesterday?'

'No, I haven't found you yet. You must try harder.' He turned away from her and sat on his stool with a stern expression.

After the tenderness of the night before Elenore felt a wave of disappointment. Peter seems distant today, yesterday he seemed so close to me, she thought.

The memory of the sensation she felt as his eyes seemed to ravish her was still fresh. His hands so searching. She looked at his face as he pinned a new sheet of paper to the easel. He seemed so determined but distant. She was no longer sure of him.

Peter said, 'New pose.'

She sat on a chair and placed her chin on her hand.

'Charming,' Peter said and smiled.

After some minutes he again said, 'New pose.'

The morning progressed and Elenore tried many poses. Noon came and went, but today, Peter made no move to stop the session.

In the mid afternoon Peter said, 'Alright, we had better stop and eat something.'

He shook his head as he put his pastel down and walked over to the kitchen.

Elenore put on her robe on and followed him. He stood by the counter and took a loaf of bread out and began to hack off pieces with a knife. She stood close to him and put her hand on his shoulder. Her breast brushed against his arm.

'Are you disappointed in me today Peter?'

'No darling, It's me, I feel apart from you. Yesterday we were so close, but today, you seem as far away as ever. It's as though we are still separated by that ocean of time.'

Elenore tightened her fingers into his shoulder and pressed her body to his, 'We are together, let's be together,' she whispered.

Peter moved away from her and continued to prepare food for them, They ate in silence until peter said, 'New pose, I want you to reach out to me, give me everything, I need to posses you.'

Elenore pushed away from him, she felt scorned. 'You don't really want to know me. You just want to torment me.'

She struck a pose. Her face became twisted in anger. Peter drew quickly but soon demanded a new pose and another, new pose, new pose.

'You must give me more. You're hiding, reveal your self to me,' Peter demanded.

Exhausted, eventually neither the painter nor Elenore could do more. Elenore put her clothes on and looked at the painter. He looked away.

'Peter, I won't come tomorrow, you don't want me.'

'You can't abandon me, not again. We needed this tension today. Creating art is like giving birth, you have to push. It can be excruciating. But I promise you tomorrow we will make progress.'

'Today you were trying to hurt me, brush me aside,'

'I would never hurt you. I need you. This will be my masterpiece, my legacy. I promise tomorrow will be better. You will see.'

'Alright Peter, if I am here tomorrow we can continue. If I don't arrive at 10, you must let me be,' she said slamming the door and ran down the stairs.

Gregor was already home when she arrived. She did not tell him about the day, but he felt that something was wrong.

'I don't want you to see the painter again,' he said.

'You're right, I don't want to go any more.' she assured him.

'Was he cruel to you? Did he touch you? I'm going to go and see him right now!'

'No, no leave him be. The experience is just too intense for me. He's striving for something that can't be achieved. He wants some perfect being, something that I am not. I can't sit for him again, he's too demanding,' she said.

But the next morning Gregor went to work at the art school as usual. When it came time for her to go to the studio she found herself walking out the door.

She arrived on time, but today she was not happy and she slumped herself down on the sofa. She put one hand behind her head and the other on her lap. Her legs slightly bent and her torso turned towards Peter.

She felt rejected, and her eyes were filled with bitterness. But soon her face took on a defiant, independent glare. She tried to cover up her real feelings, but her lips trembled, beyond her control. A sad smile came across her face as her feelings turned to tenderness, a soft pain as if her lover had gone away.

Peter, watched as her face transfigured before him, telling a story that he read like a poem. He said, 'Keep that expression, keep it, don't move.'

He picked up his small pad and moved closer to her. He drew her face then tore the page from the pad, threw it behind him and started again. Several times he tore the page off the pad and started afresh. Eventually, he stopped and looked at what he had captured and smiled.

'What's the matter Peter? Can I move now?' she said

'What's the matter? Nothing at all. Yes, you can move, but remember that expression it was perfect.'

Elenore, felt relieved, after yesterday she wanted this to be the last session.

'I'm so happy Peter that at last you have got something. Is it enough, do you still need me?'

'Yes darling I still need you. But perhaps I have something I can work with now. Take up the pose from the other day again. Try to put that expression back on your face, but I have that at least, in my head and on paper. It is just how I remember you, that night.'

'What do you mean remember me?'

'Never mind, just take up that pose. But relax, this will take a while.

Elenore lay back on the sofa again and tried to remember her pose.

Peter moved about the studio quickly opening the drawers of a large plan chest. He rummaged through drawers of paper until he found what he wanted. He pulled out a large piece of thick paper and pinned it to the board on the easel.

He picked up a pastel and stood ready to draw. 'Come on, get the pose correct, and that expression, please, remember how you felt.'

Elenore bent her legs and twisted her torso. She tried to remember how bittersweet, insecure, and afraid she had felt but it was hard. Now that Peter was happy, so was she. Instead of spurned she felt delighted that they were making progress.

The two hours passed but Peter kept drawing. He glanced at the clock and said, 'You can't leave yet. Have a break, but today we must keep going until I have captured you.'

Peter continued drawing her in the same pose until late afternoon when he let her return home.

Pleased with his work he went to pour himself a glass of wine, but the bottle was empty. He put on his beret and picked up a bag and walked to the supermarket to buy more wine.

Peter had given up drinking some years ago. It seemed to distract him from his work, and he wanted nothing to get in his way. But now, he wanted to relax, to ponder his creation. He hadn't had feelings of this kind for so long. It was as if he was young again. The world seemed full of hope and promise and he dared to dream about the future.

'Yes my dear,' he said out loud, 'Now we are together again, nothing will make us part.'

He sat at his table transfixed by the image on his easel, sipping his wine he smiled, imagining the finished painting. In his mind he mixed every colour, painted every stroke. He realised that he would need more paint and a canvas, he decided to go to the artists supply shop first thing in the morning before the next session.

The next morning he put on his beret and walked over to the artist suppliers on Bilderdijkstraat. The door chime played it's off key melody as Peter walked into the empty shop.

This was the oldest and best artist suppliers in Amsterdam. The family run business had been in this location for generations. The cavernous store was filled with the finest paints, chalks, papers and top quality canvases. Peter had spent many happy hours there thumbing through all the materials and assessing their quality. He could loose himself in the shop and not leave for hours.

He often came across fellow artists, who like him were wandering through the shop, and they would talk at length. The shop assistant would be sent to fetch them coffee from the cafe next door. In the old days they would smoke cigarettes and more besides. Sometimes customers would meander to the back of the shop to find half a dozen bleary eyed artists sitting on stools gesticulating their hands and talking feverishly about art and life.

The shop was run by his friend Jens, the great-great-grandson of the original owner. He had an encyclopedic knowledge of everything in stock. The materials they were made from, where and how they were made, and which artists preferred this or that.

Soon Jens emerged from the store room. 'Hey Peter, what do you need today?' he said.

'I need a large stretched canvas. Two metres wide.'

'You mean a life size canvas, for a figure painting? How exciting. I can prepare one for you in say, two days.'

'No no, I need one right now. I have a vision. I must get it down quickly before it fades. Show me what you have in stock.'

'Yes master, of course, what ever you need.' said Jens.

He took Peter to the store room where he rummaged through prepared canvases that were stacked against the wall. At last he said, 'Ah ha, this is perfect, I will have this one.'

'I'm sorry, you can't take that canvas. It's a special order and it's being collected today.'

Peter glared at Jens, and he understood the urgency.

'But for you master, that customer can wait. What else do you need?'

'Paint, lots of paint.'

He carried the canvas, unwrapped, in both hands with a large bag full of tubes of oil paint back to the studio and struggled up the narrow staircase.

Opening the studio door with his left hand while holding the large canvas in his other he entered and placed the canvas on the easel.

Soon, Elenore arrived and undressed. 'So you are starting the canvas today Peter?' she asked.

'Yes dear, it is time for us to begin in earnest. Please resume the pose.'

Peter had pinned up the various sketches and studies he had made around the room. He picked a soft pencil and looking at Elenore he began to draw her outline on the canvas.

'Oh darling, you look so beautiful today. I'm so looking forward to our big day,' said the painter.

'Our big day? Asked Elenore, 'You mean when the painting is finished?'

Peter didn't seem to hear her but kept mumbling to himself. His face became animated with smiles and frowns. He strained his ear as if he couldn't quite make out what someone was saying, then nodded his head as if he now understood.

All the while Elenore kept her pose. After half an hour Peter said, 'Ten minute rest.'

Peter busied himself mixing paints and choosing brushes. After the break she resumed her pose, and he applied his first strokes of paint to the canvas.

As the afternoon sun began to draw long shadows across the studio and the light slipped away from her body in a sharp dark line. Peter said, 'Enough for today.'

As she was leaving he touched her hand and enveloped her in his arms. 'Darling, you are so wonderful. I can't wait until you return.'

Elenore felt an unease as she walked home. Gregor was waiting for her when she opened the door.

'How did it go today? He asked.

'Peter is progressing fast now. He's started painting the canvas. But now he worries me in a different way. He seems strangely removed. As if he is in another time and place.'

The next morning as Elenore entered the studio, she noticed that the canvas was covered by a sheet.

'You don't want me to see the painting Peter?'

'No my darling, no one can see it until it is finished.'

She resumed her pose and Peter painted.

'Painting is like sculpting in clay,' Peter said, 'You apply a bit here, then there. If you put too much in one place, you take it off and add more where needed. Eventually, the subject emerges. Painting with oil is infinitely malleable, you just keep making changes until you're satisfied.'

'How do you know when you are finished Peter?'

'I never finish a painting. They are simply taken away from me and sold, and I have no further access to them.'

He continued painting, applying layers of light, dark and shadow, filling in the spaces. By the end of the day a definite female form had begun to grow on the canvas.

'Oh darling, I am beginning to see you now, yes you are coming through nicely. You are beautiful my love.'

Elenore had been holding the same pose for two days now and her mind kept drifting off. She had to reminded herself periodically where she was. She heard Peter's voice and presumed he was talking to her. But she looked at him and he seemed distant, as if in another place entirely.

'So you are pleased with progress Peter? She said. But he didn't seem to hear her.

'Peter, is it alright if I leave now? It's getting late?'

'Of course darling, you must do what you need to do.'

She stretched and yawned and got up to put her clothes on. Peter didn't stop painting, and when she walked to the door she said, 'Peter, are you well? Are you alright?'

'Oh yes, I haven't been this happy for so long, it's so wonderful to be with you.'

'Do you want me to come back tomorrow or do you have everything you need now Peter?'

'Humm, what? Oh yes, I have everything I need now. I have no need of anything more.'

'Very well then. Perhaps I will come back in a few days to see how you are progressing. What do you say?

'Of course darling, of course.'

Elenore walked home unsure if Peter had heard what she had said or not.

'How was the painter today?' asked Gregor.

'I'm worried about him. It's as if he's not there at all.'

'So the painting has stopped?'

'No, on the contrary, he painted furiously all day. He barely took his eyes off the canvas, even when I got up to rest or eat. He didn't seem to notice whether I was there at all. But he kept talking to me. Most of the time I couldn't keep track of what he was saying.'

'Does he want you again tomorrow?'

'No he says he has all he needs now. I said I would go back to check on his progress in a few days.'

'Thank goodness,' said Gregor. I'm glad it's over. I hope the painting turns out to be the masterpiece he wants. How is it looking anyway?'

'I haven't seen it at all. He keeps it covered or turned away from me. He says no one can see it until it's finished.'

'Well he is the painter, and it's his painting,' said Gregor.

7

Peter didn't notice that Elenore had left him. He kept painting, adding a stroke here and another there. He mixed colours on his pallet and applied a few strokes to the face or arm. Now he could see her, yes she was all there. Her smile, so sweet but sad. Her eyes had a different smile than her lips, and he realised, Of course, this was before, yes she was happy then. So changed the lips to match the eyes.

Her breasts were small now, but she was still a young woman, not a mother. Youth is to be enjoyed, and we still have so much time, he thought. He stopped to make him self dinner and ate sitting at his table staring at her, Lana. She was talking to him. It was so nice to hear her voice.

As he finished his meal and washed his plates, he heard her scolding him. She was angry now. He put down the plate and went back to the painting. He changed her eyes, her mouth, the blush on her cheek, the tension in her fingers.

But her anger didn't last, and soon she was happy again. She wanted him, lusted after him. He changed her again. Her mouth drooped down with parted moist lips. Her eyes lost in a fog of desire, passion.

Now they were in a post amorous daze, as if in a cloud. All feeling of self trans-joined in one another. One being, floating in clouds of bliss.

The painter awoke the next morning. He had no recollection of going to bed, only being with his lover entwined in her body. Her fragrant loamy scent enveloped him, his desire stirred again. But where was she? Then he heard her voice and returned to the painting.

'Ah, there you are my love. You are radiant today.'

But then she was angry again and he couldn't bear it, he snapped and shouted at her. Tormented he turned away and she was gone. 'No, no, you cannot leave me can you?'

Her soft voice soon spoke to him again. Relieved, he vowed that they would never be apart again.

Relaxed now, he continued to paint. Life flowed through her and days, months and years of time passed with each stroke of paint he applied. She matured and their lives together grew rich, full of texture and meaning. They understood each other completely and were as one.

Peter savoured his meals, sipped wine in the evening, and talked to Lana into the small hours until his eyes could stay open no more and he slept. The next morning he woke again to find his love still on the canvas and took up his brush and continued to paint.

Lost in time, wrapped in bliss. Peter persisted until with one final stroke, he stopped. He marvelled at the beauty of his painting. The sophistication of his technique. He had captured everything that Lana's life had been, her feelings of joy and loss, meaning and disenchantment. In every line of her beautiful face he could see how the years had left their marks on her. But she had come through all adversity and lived her life to the full. Here she was, perfection, beautiful, vivacious, tender and loving.

Exhausted, his empty wine glass slipped from his hand and still sitting in his chair in front of his finished masterpiece he fell into a deep slumber. Happy that at last he had achieved his goal.

Elenore had told the Museum that she was unwell and could not go to work. Having no idea how many sessions Peter would need her for, she was relieved that after only a few days she could return to her normal schedule. Gregor told her not to worry about the painter, he had a wife who would be looking after him. But as the days went by she never lost the sensation of his eyes burning her skin, his soft hands caressing her, his lips on hers.

Three days went by, and she could wait no more. After work, instead of cycling straight home she peddled over to the studio and walked up the stairs. Ding dong, the doorbell chimed. But there was no answer. She pressed her ear to the door, and she was sure she could hear talking. She rang the bell again but still no answer. She knocked on the door, and again. She listened once more. Could she hear voices, or was it her imagination?

She cycled the rest of the way home her heart pounding again, like the day the painter ignored her and hurt her.

'Gregor, I went to see Peter but he didn't answer the door,' she said.

'He didn't answer the door, or he wasn't there?'

'I think I heard voices, but I'm not sure.'

'Then don't worry Elenore, he's probably with his wife.'

After their evening meal Elenore told Gregor that she was going for a walk. She could not put Peter out of her mind, and she made her way back to the studio. She knocked and rang the bell, but there was still no response. She left confused, not knowing what to do.

She wasn't sure of the address, but when she found the street she remembered and made her way up to Elke's apartment.

She rang the bell but there was no answer there either. As she was leaving a neighbour came out of the apartment next door.

'If you are looking for Elke I am afraid that she is away for a few days,' the woman said.

'Is her husband with her do you know?' asked Elenore.

'I don't think so young lady. I believe that she has gone to Paris on her own.'

Elenore rushed back home.

'Gregor, we must find the painter, I'm so worried about him.'

'I have his phone number. I'll call him,' said Gregor.

He tried the number, but it seemed to be disconnected. Gregor rolled his eyes and said, 'Alright, we'll go to the studio together, but not now, it's too late. We'll go in the morning.'

Elke looked forward to her regular trips to Paris. She had visited several of her favourite dealers and showed them photographs of Peter's completed works from the past year. As always, they agreed to take his work on consignment that they were confident they would sell quickly.

She had telephoned Peter soon after she had arrived and he seemed perfectly fine. He said the model was very professional and that the sessions were going well. She called again the next day, and the day after and he said the same thing. But for the last three days he had not answered the telephone at all, despite her many calls.

She cut short her trip and took an early morning train from Paris to Amsterdam. The train pulled into Amsterdam Central, she made her way outside and found the number 4 tram which stopped very close to Peter's place. Soon Elke was dragging her roller bag up the stairs to the studio.

She was surprised to see a young couple waiting there with worried expressions on their faces.

'Oh, Elke I am so glad you have come. Please excuse us. We were at your soirée last week. Elenore has been modelling for Peter as I am sure you know.'

Elke looked Elenore up and down, 'You are beautiful young lady. At least my husband has taste, um, as do you ...?'

'Oh, I am Gregor, at your service.'

'Have you rung the bell?' Asked Elke?

'Yes, that's why I brought Gregor with me this time. I knocked and rang the bell yesterday and just now but he hasn't come to the door,' said Elenore.

'Allow me,' said Elke, taking out her key and opening the door.

Elke entered the studio and saw Peter slumped in his chair. She rushed to him, but was relieved.

'He's only asleep, the old fool. It seems as if he's been drinking,' she said, looking at the empty wine bottle and fallen glass. 'It's best to just let him sleep, he hasn't touched alcohol in ages.'

The three of them stood in a semicircle around the painter looking down on him. Elenore wanted to take his hand, but she held back sheepishly.

'Was it you that drove him to take up drinking again Elenore?' asked Elke.

'I, I don't know. The last sitting was a few days ago he was working furiously on the painting. He said he didn't need me any more. But he was acting very strangely, talking to himself.'

'Well, lets see how he got on with the painting,' said Elke.

They turned to look at the painting. The morning sun illuminated the studio in a perfect soft light. The large canvas was placed on the easel, and it was covered in paint.

There were dark areas and light areas. The middle section had a large thickness of grey green paint with a multitude of different strokes as if layer upon layer had been added. Perhaps there were many colours, but they had all merged into a soupy melange each one cancelling the other out.

They peered into the mass of paint, trying to discern what was there. They inched closer and closer, tiptoeing, gazing intently at the painting.

'There,' said Elenore, pointing at the canvas, 'Can't you see it? It's a smile, the one he liked the other day. He said that was the look he needed.'

Gregor and Elke peered at the painting.

Gregor said 'Oh yes, you're right, a smile, humm.'

'Ah,' said Elke. 'Yes, I can see it now, a smile.'

****

No.4

Ellie

1

The phone beside Antoine's bed buzzed and vibrated. The TV switched itself on, and soon the morning barrage of chatter, mindless stories and inane advertisements clogged his senses. The clatter made him feel alive, as if he were not alone. It made him feel as if he were a player in the world – his world, in any case – Los Angeles, the never-ending story. LA, the capital of content, music, TV and movies was the only place for someone like him to be. But today he was going to that other nirvana, the entertainment capital of the world, Lost Wages, the Neon City, the Big Motel, Las Vegas.

He gulped his coffee, pressed the garage door button, and he was out into the flow of cars, trucks and robo-taxis. His EV moved silently along from his apartment in Westwood up to Santa Monica Boulevard, and he soon reached highway 101, the Ventura Freeway. The traffic moved along the freeway as if it were an accordion being compressed, slowing down nearly to a halt, then stretching out again and moving along faster.

At one slow point, he glanced out his window on the right to see an empty car beside him. It still gave him a shiver to see a car moving with no one in the driver's seat. He looked to his left, and the car there had no driver but a passenger in the back staring at his phone as the vehicle sped up again and overtook him.

His car was an older model, and he still had the option to drive himself. He was from the age of the gas guzzlers and enjoyed driving his car. I'll switch to autopilot on the way into Las Vegas, he thought. He passed the exits for Chinatown and downtown Los Angeles and turned on to Interstate 10 before joining Interstate 15 and veering north towards San Bernadino and Barstow.

Once he was out of the congestion of Los Angeles, he began to relax. He was in no hurry. So at Baker, he turned off the freeway into the Mojave National Preserve and walked on the Teutonia Peak Trail to have a look at the Kelso Sand Dunes.

With anticipation, he climbed the rocky ridge, wanting to see the wide open landscape filled with Joshua trees once again. He loved the ancient landscape with so many geological formations and delicate desert vegetation. He could see ancient sand dunes dancing into the distance. The clarity of the air made the distances foreshortened. Were the ridges five miles away or fifty?

But the Joshua Trees were gone, burned and blown away with the wind. The great fires of the previous years had destroyed the desert vegetation. Instead of a lush, slow growing, intricate covering of desert plants, he saw the remnants of burnt, dead trees and the beginnings of invasive weeds taking over the ancient landscape.

A park sign said cheerily that since the fires had devastated the area, the park authorities were 're-imagining the Mojave...' re-imagining it without the Joshua trees.

At the top of the trail, looking across to the sand dunes, he remembered standing in the exact same spot with his father's hand on his shoulder and hearing him say, 'Antoine, never cease to wonder at the magnificence of God's creation. Always give thanks for the beauty, wonder and bounty of this world.'

As he viewed the desolation, the desecration of the land, he felt a deep sense of dread, guilt and foreboding. Quickly, he retraced his steps to the car and drove back to the freeway. Driving along Interstate 15, visions of fire and dust tormented him as the EV took him towards Las Vegas.

It was spring, and the high desert plateau had a sprinkling of snow with rain squalls swirling across the plains. The smell of sage reminded him of driving through the desert with his father. 'Open the window, Antoine, let the desert air fill your lungs. That sage-desert smell, breathe it in, humm, yes, the taste of the old world, the real world.'

His father was from Louisiana, but had moved to California with an aching in his heart after World War 2. He raised his family in what was to become Silicon Valley in the South San Francisco Bay area. There, Antoine and his siblings would trail behind their father as they hiked through the old Redwood groves of Big Basin in the Santa Cruz Mountains. But Big Basin had also been burned, laid waste, and now was a shadow of its former glory, awaiting its re-imagining.

His father was from the generation of hope and trust in the future. He had belief in the American way of life and democratic system.

Antoine was from the Cold War generation who lived with the certainty that one day the world would annihilate itself in a nuclear armageddon, '...dreaming of our damnation, night and day, it won't let up...'

Now that the nightmare of human induced catastrophe was real, everyone seemed to switch off, determined to ignore the world around them until it burned or drowned them. What else could a person do? Now was the time for consequences, and there was no choice but to hang on and survive the ride as best as one could.

By early afternoon, he approached the outskirts of Las Vegas. He switched on the autonomous drive and set the navigation for the Galatian Hotel and Casino. It is not a good idea to drive myself into the city, he thought. The possibility of one of the robo-taxis hitting his vehicle was bad enough. It would be even worse if he hit one of them. He didn't want to be embroiled with the corporations that owned them, or more accurately, their AI chatbots and virtual attorneys that would drive him to despair.

His vehicle pulled into the EV placement zone of the Galatian arrival area. A baggage delivery robot retrieved his bag and disappeared into the bowels of the building, hopefully taking it to his living environment. He had already checked in virtually with his watch on approach to the hotel.

Without having seen or had any contact with another human, he settled into his environment and ordered a pizza to be delivered by a drone to his window, the Victuals Access Point.

He looked out at the expansive view over Las Vegas Boulevard, the Strip. Just a few streets further away, the arid desert began. In the distance, the mountains that surrounded 'the Meadows', as the native people called the low lying basin of modern Las Vegas, rose up to snow covered-peaks. Air-taxis zipped along their routes between the airport and the major hotels. He looked across to the 'Sphere' with its ever changing colours and vivid displays of advertising.

A major new attraction was under construction in between the Sphere and the Galatian. It was called the 'Metasphere', and when completed, it would be a 'virtual world within a world to satisfy all imaginings and learnings in an inclusive, virtual and sustainable envelope.'

He slumped into a sofa. Now, at last, he could relax. Puffing on his vape, he remembered why he was there – because of Ellie, of course.

Ellie was about to begin a two week residency in the auditorium at the Galatian. Antoine was a musician and an audio engineer. He would be mixing the sound in the control box at the shows.

Ellie and her band had been a country rock sensation. She had three number ones, four number twos, and had sold millions of records. She could sing in any style and helped launch the careers of many artists, singing backing vocals on their records with her unmistakable voice.

She learned to sing as a girl in Tennessee. Raised as a Catholic, she sang at weddings, christenings and Mass on Sundays. From her earliest childhood, all she wanted to do was sing and entertain people.

He had not seen Ellie in a long time, not since she had left him in a storm of tears that terrible night. I'm just happy to be in Ellie's orbit again, he thought as he pulled the sweet vapour into his lungs. He relaxed, and his thoughts wandered in a tantalising haze of inspiration, paranoia and confusion.

What seemed like only moments later he shuddered awake. I'd better get myself together, there's no time to waste. I'm not getting any younger sitting here.

He ate his pizza, had a shower, closed the door of his environment, and went to find the Galatian auditorium.

2

Antoine had worked in the Galatian auditorium before, but it had since undergone a complete refit and had been renamed the Volume. It used to be a normal theatre with a stage and tiered seating in front of it. As he walked inside from the main entrance, he saw something different.

The stage was now circular and jutted out into the seating area. The auditorium had been reshaped, and behind the stage was a hemispherical dome wrapped around it, making it look like an altar in a Catholic basilica.

Enormous LED screens covered the interior of the half-dome. He walked up to the front of the stage and turned around to look at the room. It seemed as if the capacity had more than doubled with steep tiers of seating. A vast array of lights covered the ceiling, but he couldn't see any audio speakers anywhere.

Peering through the dimly lit auditorium, high up above the last tiers of seats at the back, he saw a large room with a glass window. Lights were on, and people were milling around. That must be the control box, he thought. I'd better find my way up there.

As he entered the box, he was greeted by the show director, Rodrigo. 'Hi Antoine, you'll be working here,' he said, walking him to an audio mixing console.

It was a standard mixing desk covered in illuminated switches and displays, but with a mysterious new section added to the side. Several other consoles were spread out in a semi-circular array, with Rodrigo's desk at the back.

'This is an amazing setup you have here,' said Antoine, as his eyes moved around the room.

'Well, it sure is the state of the art and the audio is just one part of it. These other consoles are for lights and video projection onto the big screens, hologram projection, haptics and atmospherics, outside video feeds, and social media integration.

'We have a broadcast facility with live feeds to and from studios, and a large array of remote cameras set up all through the Volume. The stage can rotate and move up and down, you name it, we got it. We're still getting used to it. Ellie is going to be the first act to play here since the upgrade,' Rodrigo said.

'It looks amazing, but where are the speakers? I guess the audio hasn't been set up yet,' said Antoine.

'Sure, the audio is installed. We have immersive sound with spatial audio capabilities and a matrix array of speakers. They're all hidden behind the LED screens and throughout the theatre. You're going to like the sound. It'll be better than you've ever heard.

'The speakers can digitally aim sound at specific spots in the audience with consistent volume to every seat in the venue. So whether you are in the front row or right up at the back, the sound will be the same volume and texture. When Ellie whispers into her microphone, everyone in the audience will hear her like she's talking to them personally.'

'There are so many lights in the ceiling, I've never seen such a complicated set up before,' said Antoine.

'There are over 1,000 lights up there. We also have 4D features. I mean we can send out scent and wind. Each seat is rigged with haptics, that is, we can make the seat shake and vibrate. All of this will be controlled and evolved by our AI engine. We've never gone this far before. We haven't had the right artist. But everyone loves Ellie. Everyone wants to caress her, smell her, hear her whisper sweet nothings in their ears – the guys and the girls.'

'Aren't Ellie's audience a bit old for this? They're our age, not teenagers,' said Antoine.

'Well, I think that's why the promoter thought it would work for Ellie. The younger audiences are too wild, and it might all go over their heads. Anyway, this is an experiment, we're throwing everything at this one. It's a test case, and we'll learn a lot from this gig.'

Rodrigo nodded in satisfaction and pride at all the technology he had at his disposal. He looked around the box, admiring the whole setup.· 'Yup, this is bleeding edge, we're going to have a fun two weeks with Ellie,' he said, with a tear welling up in his eye.

The next day, Antoine went back to the Volume to meet his co-workers for sound checks and rehearsals. He sat down at his desk and was about to munch into a purple doughnut. He glanced down at the stage as Ellie walked on, and his heart jumped.

She was wearing a long black flowing dress. Her long red hair was draped across her shoulders. She stood in the middle of the stage and looked up at the control box. Her eyes beamed, and her red lips puckered in her romantic smile.

He thought he had finally gotten over Ellie, but his feelings for her flooded back, like a sluice gate opening. What they had was like a precious dream. They could never go back to that place again. It was over and he knew it. But seeing her now, he was overwhelmed with a desire to hold her in his arms again. He put his doughnut down and rushed to the stage.

'Hey Ellie, good to see you,' he said out of breath after the run down the stairs and across the Volume.

Ellie turned towards him and smiled. 'Hey Antoine, it's been a while, but you look just the same,' she said.

'Ellie, you sure look great. I'm working on the show with you. So you know, I thought I should say hi.'

'Of course, Antoine. I knew you were in the crew. It's nice to see you. This is a great room, isn't it?'

A man walked across the stage and hugged Ellie and said, 'Ellie, we finally made it, here we are. What a room this is, eh? This is going to be a career defining two weeks. You wait and see.'

Ellie embraced him but looked over his shoulder at Antoine, and her eyes rolled upwards. 'Thanks, I'm so glad to be here, but give me a minute, please.'

Ellie untwined herself from the man and said, 'This is the show promoter, Abe. Listen, it's nice to see you, Antoine, but I had better go now.'

'No problem, Ellie. Maybe we can have a coffee or something while we're here in Vegas?' he asked hopefully.

'Maybe, maybe, Antoine,' she replied, walking into the shadow with Abe.

Antoine watched her recede into the darkness. He felt an urge to follow them, disquieted by Ellie's look. Then he felt a strange, shaking vibration. It seemed to be coming from under the stage. He looked down at his feet and saw his shoes were vibrating. A stage electrician walked by, and he asked, 'Hey, where's the vibration coming from?'

'They're building a tunnel from the Metasphere to the Strip. It's going right underneath the Volume.'

Antoine went back up to the control box, but now that he had noticed the vibration, he couldn't escape it. It seemed to grow louder and stronger as the day went on. In the late afternoon, Rodrigo walked by his desk, and he asked, 'Rodrigo, can you hear and feel that drilling?'

'Yeah, Antoine, they're digging the next stage of the Loop car tunnel. Don't worry, they'll be quiet while the shows are on,' he said.

Antoine hoped he was right, as the vibration made it impossible for him to make a true sound evaluation. It was only two days before the first show, and after working all day, he wasn't confident at all.

Back in his environment, Antoine puffed on his vape and slumped into the sofa. His thoughts drifted back to sensuous nights spent with Ellie in his arms. You're the only one, she had said. He had believed her. He felt the same about her, but then they split up that terrible night. What a fool I was, he thought.

3

Ellie woke up, stretched out her arms and yawned. She pushed a button on the remote, and the electric blinds on the picture window in front of her bed began to purr and wind open. She lay there for a few minutes, admiring the view. Her penthouse suite in the Galatian looked down the Strip past the Bellagio and Paris hotels and on out to the desert and mountains beyond. She pulled herself up out of bed, and soon the breakfast machine arrived. She sat down to eat. The machine buzzed, and a robotic arm served her coffee with bacon and eggs.

She had performed in Las Vegas many times before. Oh, she remembered the first time, how could she ever forget the experience? She was the warm up act at the Riviera. 'Crazy Girls', a topless revue, were the main act, and backstage the girls raced around nearly naked, adjusting their G-strings and nipple tassels. It was an easy room to play, she remembered. The audience was jovial and excited. They were willing to give her a chance as they waited to see the revue.

This gig was different, she was the one and only act for two whole weeks. Elton John had advised her about playing in Las Vegas, and said, 'You have to love the audience. They're there because they think they love you.'

Las Vegas audiences were not hard to schmaltz up to, but they were hard to love, she mused.

They were a melting pot of all of American society, with a slew of Canadians, Mexicans and whoever else was in town that particular night. Ellie preferred playing at venues closer to her home back east in Tennessee. She liked the intimacy of a small venue, where the audience actually knew her music and where she was from, rather than the illusion of intimacy her promoter favoured.

Abe was an impresario, looking for performers to fill certain slots in the schedule of concerts. He wanted archetypes that he could mould, typecast into a role, like a circus master. He thought of her as a country singer serving up a standard mix of love songs and dance numbers, nothing more.

Ellie had been on the road for years playing concerts up, down and across the USA. She loved being on the road and moving from town to town. The audience didn't have time to get too close, and if she met anyone she didn't want to see, she was leaving soon anyway. In between the near constant touring, she retreated to her Malibu home to relax and recuperate on the beach.

Abe had convinced her that this two week stint in Vegas would propel her to a new career high. He talked enthusiastically about the bleeding edge technology in the Volume. He promised her that the intimacy of a small venue could be replicated in a large auditorium, and that she would reach new audiences in an unparalleled media convergence experience.

What on earth had made me believe any of his bullshit? she wondered. Well, here I am, staring out at the desert, crunching dry, salty bacon, slurping bad coffee, and wearing a t-shirt with my hair all messed up. I'd better take a shower and get to the rehearsal.

The shower was in the centre of a large marble-floored bathroom surrounded by glass on all four sides. Standing naked, she felt vulnerable, like a goldfish in a bowl.

Water pulsed from jets in the ceiling, sideways from the walls, and upwards from holes in the floor like a car wash. She struggled to stop the high powered streams of scalding water. Eventually, having figured out how to turn the water off, she sat down at an out-sized vanity wrapped in a towel.

She pressed the buttons on the remote, and the aircon switched off and on, the lights flashed, until finally, the blinds on the windows purred and rolled down. She wanted some peace from the view of the desert. She already missed her secluded beach house at Malibu. It was the only place she felt she could be herself, not on show, not a made up person, but just Ellie.

She wrapped her wet hair up in a towel and began to put on her makeup. She remembered meeting Antoine at the Volume. She liked being with him, he was uncomplicated. She could relate to him because, like her, he was a musician. She had seen his name on the list of people working on the show but had put it out of her mind. Oh, Antoine, she thought, you were always so sweet. What a great guitar player he is. I wish he could be in my band again, she sighed. Oh, why can't old lovers ever be friends?'

When she was young, she fell in love easily. But the men she knew always wanted to be the drivers in the relationship. She tried her best, but soon enough, she would find herself drifting away down her own path. She had no desire to make them follow her and was happy for them to be successful. But men, well, they have trouble playing second fiddle to a talented woman. They go berserk, or turn into cry babies if they can't be in control, she thought.

It wasn't Antoine's fault that they had split up. She simply did not feel that she could be responsible for their relationship any longer. What he called 'that terrible night' was, in her eyes, just a matter of being honest in acknowledging her own true self. She had her own path to follow.

Well, here she was years later, all alone in the world with no one to call her own. There were plenty of men who would like to lay claim to her. Well, maybe not Antoine, he was never like that. He was, I have to admit it, just in love with me. I loved him too. A tear filled her eye. I'd better stop that at once, she thought. She dabbed her eye with a tissue and thought, I mustn't let the mascara run.

Dread filled her heart. Everyone in show business passes through Vegas on their way to LA or going back to New York. Who knows who might crawl out of the woodwork to haunt me?

She finished dressing and took on her stage persona. Oh well, here I go, she thought, two weeks in Vegas, and waited patiently for the elevator to arrive.

Antoine had arrived at the Volume early. He wanted to make sure his setup was working and the sound was the way it was supposed to be. Ellie was scheduled for a full rehearsal from mid-morning. The trouble was, he wasn't at all sure how the audio setup worked.

His mixing desk now included a whole new section that he had never seen until the day before. It had controls for the sound in different seating sections, rows and even each individual seat. What am I supposed to do with this? He knew how to mix sound for a large auditorium, how to use the speakers to bring the sound close to the stage, and other speakers to throw the sound to the back. But in the Volume, the speakers were everywhere. They were in the ceiling, the walls, under the seats, in the backs of the seats, in front of the stage. How was he supposed to figure out what sounded good in each position? He couldn't sit in each seat and check the sound.

He decided that all he could do was mix the sound as he always did. He could make it sound good in the front and at the back of the auditorium, and hope for the best. By the time Ellie arrived on stage, he was ready to go – with his fingers crossed.

But then the rumbling started again. It was like a jackhammer thumping under a pile of mattresses. It didn't sound to him as if it was coming from under the volume. It seemed to be coming through the walls.

Rodrigo was seated at his desk behind Antoine. Ellie and her band arrived and waited on stage. Rodrigo spoke into his microphone. The various crews stopped to listen, including Ellie and her band.

'Listen up everyone, we are going to take this from the top as if this were the real show. I will have final control of the sound, lights and everything with the aid of our AI engine. You all look after your sections, and the AI will mix it all together and make it work in sync.'

Ellie looked mystified. Antoine put his hands on his head and exhaled. Oh boy, what are we in for? he thought.

Rodrigo bellowed, 'OK Ellie, walk back on stage and play your first number.'

Ellie walked off the stage and a few moments later came back on with her trademark Gibson J200 acoustic guitar strapped across her shoulder. Her band – keyboard player, drummer, guitarist and bassist – were all ready to start playing.

'She smiled and spoke with her birdsong voice into the microphone. 'Hi y'all, it's great to be back in Las Vegas. I'd like to play you a song that I wrote. It's a love song titled 'Please Explain'.'

She strummed her guitar and started to sing a sweet song. The band joined in softly, one by one, and the beautiful ballad drifted around the Volume. When she had finished, Rodrigo gave a sigh of relief. So far, so good thought Antoine. The first number was out of the way, and it sounded fine.

Then Ellie spoke into the mic again and said, 'This next one will get your heart thumpin' and feet stompin'. It's titled 'Wrecking Wall.'

The band started playing a fast and loud country rock number with drums pounding, guitars howling, keyboards thumping and Ellie singing her heart out.

Antoine was turning knobs furiously, pushing sliders and tapping buttons. The lead guitar was too loud and the drums echoed, bouncing off the walls, and he could hardly hear Ellie. He turned around and looked at Rodrigo with panic in his eyes. Rodrigo said, 'Ride her, Antoine, just keep going. The AI engine will kick in and fix it. Just keep going.'

Rodrigo turned to the other consoles and said to the operators, 'OK, lights, haptics, videos, hologram, atmos. Start your routines.'

Lights flashed all around the volume in a blinding array of colours. The empty seats began to shake like massage chairs. Dry ice billowed across the stage, obscuring Ellie. The huge LED screens showed distorted images of Ellie and videos of desert vistas, waterfalls and horses galloping. In front of the stage, a hologram of Ellie hovered in the air, distorted and flickering. The stage shuddered, and began to rotate. The drummer's hi-hat toppled, and Ellie almost fell off the stage.

Eventually, the song came to a thundering climax, and Antoine collapsed onto his desk, covered in sweat.

Rodrigo said softly into the mic. 'Um... Ellie, that was great. We'll take five now... um, I think we need to make some adjustments to the setup. You and the band grab a cup of coffee... OK, sweetheart?'

Ellie turned on her heels and stormed off the stage, whipped the guitar from her shoulders, and threw it to a roadie. Fuming, she slammed the door of her dressing room and fell into a chair.

There was a tap tap on the door, 'Can I come in, honey?' Abe, the promoter whispered. The door cracked open, and his face poked in.

'OK sweetheart?' she said.

Abe smiled and came into the room.

'That was a disaster. Who is that guy? I was nearly thrown off the stage – a hurricane wind tried to blow me away. I was blinded by flashing lights and suffocated by smoke. What was that horrible chemical smell? If that guy calls me sweetheart again I'm gonna ...'

'Ellie, Ellie, calm down. It'll work itself out. That's what rehearsals are for,' said Abe.

'RE-HEAR-SAL over! What about the sound mix? I thought Antoine was working on this show. What the hell was he doing up there? You should fire the bunch of them, starting with Antoine. I'm going back to my hotel. The rest of you morons can figure it out. You're all trying to destroy my career!'

The room vibrated, and they could hear a drilling sound. 'What is that vibration and noise? This is the worst venue I have ever been in. I think we should cancel the show,' she said.

'Don't worry, Ellie, the drilling won't be going on during the shows. Look, I'm going to go see Rodrigo and get all the technical issues sorted out. You're right, you don't need to do any more. Go back to your suite and relax,' said Abe.

Ellie walked through the stage door of the Volume and out to the Galatian casino. She had to stop and orientate herself. She strained to see across the expanse of the casino and wondered, where exactly is the elevator to my suite? Oh yes, it's over there

She walked around the end of the gaming floor, past the slots and restaurants. But then she stopped in her tracks and felt the blood drain from her face. She saw a familiar figure. Yes, it was Jack. standing on an escalator going up.

When she realised he was heading away from her, she regained her composure. My God, she thought, Jack is here. I guess I knew he would be. Who else is going to show up? she wondered. She continued on to her elevator and went up to her suite, and poured herself a brandy.

She hadn't seen Jack for a long time and had finally gotten him out of her system. Of course he's in Las Vegas, she thought. He always shows up, like a bad penny. She had known Jack since before she had made her first recording. She was playing in a small club, and he came backstage to meet her after the show. They were lovers from then on.

She swore to herself time and again that she would stop seeing him. But whenever he showed up, she remembered the feeling and felt a tingling sensation on the back of her neck. She fell for him every time. He would only ever be around for a few days, then he would be gone. He never told her where he was going or where he had come from. He always said, 'You know I'm in business. I have to travel all over the place. I'll see you soon, somewhere along the trail.'

'Don't come back, Jack. I try to forget you, forget our time together. Just when I've got you out of my heart, you come back again.'

'Ah, Ellie, I know you don't mean that. You know I'll always be your Jack of Hearts.'

She was sure he would appear as if out of nowhere, backstage, or in her dressing room as he always did. But does he know I've seen him here in Vegas? It would be just like Jack to have timed things so that he would be going up that escalator as I walked by. Yes, he must know that I saw him. He doesn't leave anything to chance.

There was another bad penny that she now realised she was not going to be able to avoid, Tom Diamon. She had managed to drive him out of her memory. He hadn't been in the newspapers or on TV for years now. She had hoped that he had recast himself as a reclusive billionaire, keeping out of the limelight. But no, no, not Tom. He will surely come after me as well, show up somewhere, backstage or even here in my room.

She poured another drink and curled up on the sofa. I wish Antoine were here right now to protect me. He was the only one who ever really cared about me. Tears filled her eyes, and her mascara began to run.

Ellie fell asleep on the sofa and woke up a couple of hours later. She felt confident again as she switched on the coffee machine. I'm a star, she reminded herself, a star, and they are just pests, all these men buzzing around me like flies. I don't need them, and I don't want them. I'm not going to stoop to their level. No, I'll rise above the fray.

She felt like a new person, strong and determined. They don't know me. They love some fake creature they have created that they pretend is me. She felt that she needed a change of image and picked up the house phone and booked an appointment in the beauty parlour.

I want something different, she told the hairdresser, completely different. She didn't want to be a redhead anymore. Soon her long hair had been cut short. She sat with her head all wrapped up, waiting for the new hair colour to set in. As she waited, her thoughts turned to her family in Tennessee. She hardly ever saw her mother and father. She wanted to go home. She would; after these two weeks I'll go straight home, she thought.

She remembered Camille, Tom's wife. Poor Camille, she was always so polite and thoughtful. She is a very bright woman, it's such a shame that she got captured by a man like Tom. I hope she'll be all right. She tried to think about anything and everything, but eventually her mind came back to Jack. It always happens this way, I just can't get him off my mind, she thought. But she was determined this time, determined to get rid of Jack and Tom once and for all.

When her hair was finished, she made another appointment to have her makeup done before the first show and went back to her suite. She opened the door, and saw a giant bouquet of flowers on the dining table with a with a note from Tom. So, he's going to come backstage after the show? She went to her suitcase, which was only half unpacked, and fumbled around, rummaging through socks and blouses until she found the small, hard case she was looking for. She opened it, took out the hardware, and put it in her purse.

She picked up her phone and texted Zachary, her lead guitarist and musical director. Hey Zachary, come on over to my suite right away. I want to talk to you about the show.

4

Rodrigo tried to figure out what had gone wrong. 'The AI engine was supposed to sync it all together. We're going to have to come up with better prompts,' he said. But when Abe arrived in the control box grim-faced, Rodrigo was left with little choice.

'Ellie doesn't like the wind, smoke or smells. She doesn't want the stage to rotate. She doesn't want all the seats shaking like massage chairs. She doesn't care if every seat can have its own ambience and sound attenuation. She DOES want the sound to be GOOD. Do you all understand? Especially you, Rodrigo, and you, Antoine,' he said, giving a final open eyed glare at Antoine.

Rodrigo was very upset. 'With all this technology at my command, this was going to be my biggest success, all ruined by that damn AI engine,' he said.

By the end of the day, many of the state of the art features available to Rodrigo had been switched off.

Antoine and the sound team spent the rest of the day re-configuring the sound system to work more like a normal concert setup. They switched off most of the 1,000 speakers dispersed around the venue and instead put everything through speakers near the stage, projecting sound into the seats like a normal show. Antoine got roadies to sit in seats all over the auditorium and report on the sound quality.

After 12 hours of reconfiguration and sound tests, Antoine was exhausted. I need a drink, he thought, and headed out into the Galatian casino. He walked past the box office and pushed the exit door open. He was confronted by a sea of gambling tables across a vast room. Hundreds of slot machines ringed the main gambling floor with flashing lights and the ringing of electronic bells and whistles. Restaurants and bars circled the floor, and corridors the size of city streets turned off in all directions.

He had no idea which way to go. He decided to simply walk across the huge room, right through the middle, and see what was on the other side.

He walked through banks of flashing, beeping slots, each with a large person crouched in front of it pushing buttons. He went down a few steps onto the main floor of gambling tables.

Roulette, blackjack, baccarat, craps and poker tables were crowded in. The floor was buzzing with gamblers placing bets and croupiers gathering in piles of chips. Waitresses in scanty outfits rushed to and fro delivering drinks and food to the mass of gamblers.

Eventually he made his way to the other side and climbed the steps up to the banks of slots. He saw a corridor with a street sign with arrows pointing to various destinations within the complex. The main hotels on the Strip were connected by a series of corridors and overpasses. It was possible to spend an entire evening wandering from one to another without ever going outside. It was disorientating, and after a while, Antoine had no idea which hotel he was in.

He came to a crossroads and a sign pointing left, to Paris. He turned in that direction and walked down a long corridor lined with clothing stores, Gucci, Versace and other top-end brands. Escalators went up and down, and corridors led off to left and right. Eventually he found himself in the foyer of the Paris Hotel and Casino. Now enervated as well as exhausted, he walked into the Paris bar. A waiter asked him if he would prefer to be inside or outside. He needed fresh air, and asked the waiter to show him out to a table on the balcony.

The balcony looked across the Strip to the enormous Bellagio hotel complex with a large fountain in a lake at its entrance. People streamed past below on the Strip.

It was dark now, and flood lights beamed onto the facade of Bellagio as a pyrotechnic display threw coloured rockets into the air. He looked up over his shoulder to see the Eiffel Tower - or the Las Vegas version of it, anyway - soaring above him, bathed in red, white and blue lights. The towers of The Cosmopolitan and the Aria hotels sparkled in the distance further down the Strip.

His Irish and soda arrived, and he asked the waiter to bring him another one. He was familiar with the Strip, but this time he felt overwhelmed by the volume of people. He often wondered why anyone wanted to go on vacation in what was nothing more than a giant shopping mall. Was it the gambling – the implied possibility of winning – that they liked? But it wasn't really gambling. After all, who really won at the tables or slots in Las Vegas? No one except the house. They made sure of that.

After a few drinks, he felt relaxed and turned his attention to the people in the bar. He recognised someone – yes, it was Jack, Ellie's Jack. They caught each other's eyes, and Antoine smiled and raised his glass.

Jack was a strange guy, thought Antoine. He never said much but always seemed to know something you didn't. At least, that was the impression he gave, as if he were smarter than you, one step ahead. He looked again, and Jack was gone. Humm, he was there just a second ago. He looked around, but nope, he was gone.

Antoine had met both Jack and Ellie when he got a short term job playing guitar in her band for a tour of the Southwest. At that time, Ellie was involved with Jack. After the first show, she and Antoine talked for a long while. She seemed to like him. 'You're so sweet, Antoine, and you play great guitar,' she said. She stared into his eyes, her face so full of life.

From that night on, he couldn't get her out of his mind. By the end of the tour, they were lovers. But she said she didn't leave Jack for him. No, she only saw Jack when they both happened to be in the same town at the same time, and it was over now.

Nevertheless, Jack hung around, like a dirty shirt. He would show up every now and then, at concerts and parties. Whenever Jack was in town, Antoine went into despair. He knew Ellie still had feelings for her 'Jack of Hearts'. 'Oh, don't be silly, Antoine. I would never cheat on you, not with Jack or anybody. I'm with you now. I love you, you're the only one.'

Nobody was sure where Jack's money came from, but he seemed to be wealthy. People said he was an early backer of a Silicon Valley unicorn – a multi-billion dollar tech company. But no one ever said which one, and everything about him was a mystery.

Now, after several whiskey and sodas, Antoine was merrier than he had been when he first arrived. He tilted his head back to finish the last sips of his drink before heading back to his room in the Galatian. The bar tender plonked a fresh drink down in front of him. 'This one's on the house,' he said with a smile. Typical Las Vegas, the longer they keep you, the more you end up spending or losing at the tables, thought Antoine.

He finished his free drink and, now decidedly drunk, wandered around the casino looking for an exit. After some time he found himself back in the Galatian casino. He caught a glimpse of a silver haired man walking with two other people. My God, it's Tom Diamon, he thought. But I guess it's no surprise. Tom does own the Galatian.

The group moved quickly through the room to a waiting elevator and a doorman ushered them in. The doors closed, and they were gone.

He had met Tom years ago. Ellie had introduced him after a concert one night. Curious to find out where Tom was going, he walked up to the elevator, but the doorman said, 'Sir, you can't use this elevator, it's private.'

Behind his shoulder he heard the unmistakable voice of Jack. 'It's all right, he's with me,' he said.

'Yes sir,' said the doorman, and he pushed the elevator button.

Antoine turned to see Jack, smiling, 'Hi Antoine, it's been a long time I guess,' he said.

The elevator arrived and they went in. The doorman turned and stretching his arm into the car, pushed a button on the inside panel and said 'Have a good evening, gentlemen.'

The doors swished closed, and the elevator accelerated upward. 'Thanks Jack. Where are we going?'

Jack smiled and half laughed, dropping his head. His eyes turned up to look directly at Antoine, 'The high rollers casino, where else?' he said.

The elevator made a ping, and came to a halt. The doors opened, and a doorman stood with his hands clasped in front of him. 'This way gentlemen,' he said.

He ushered them into a large penthouse with floor-to-ceiling windows on all sides looking out onto the Strip far below. The room had several gambling tables and a bar at one end, 'Let's get a drink and watch the fun,' said Jack.

They sat down on stools, and the bartender served them. Tom was at a table at the farthest end of the room. The table was up three shallow steps and partly obscured by Japanese-style blinds. Waitresses dressed in kimonos floated around serving drinks. Six overly tanned men sat at the table looking at the cards in their hands. Opulent and self-assured, these were the highest of the high rollers.

Tom was at the furthest point of the table with his back to the wall. Behind him stood an elegantly dressed Asian woman and a lean, hard-faced man with an earpiece visible, his hands clasped in front of him. Next to

Tom sat a woman who looked bored, as if she had been there before and wanted to go home. Younger than Tom, she had obviously been a great beauty in her youth. She still was beautiful, elegant, and refined. But her expression told a story of neglect and disappointment. She looked like an accoutrement, something necessary but taken for granted. Her name was Camille.

She was Tom's wife, and some said she was his most valuable asset. She came from a cultured East Coast family. She was a talented writer, or had been until she met Tom. She was known for being courteous and genuine, with a good heart.

Tom was another of Ellie's old lovers. She didn't like to talk about him. 'That old lizard, I should never have had anything to do with him. I was so young and had just had my first hit record. I should have been more careful getting involved with someone like that. He wanted to own me,' she said.

Tom looked happy. He was at the top of the table, the highest of the high rollers. As the man in control, he was the centre of attention. This was his casino, and he knew he was going to win this poker game. He always won.

One of the reddish-brown men threw his cards down on the table and laughed out loud. Tom laughed even louder as the dealer raked the mound of gambling chips from the middle of the table towards him.

All the men laughed and drank from large crystal goblets. The dealer indicated a break, and the players stood up and chatted with each other.

Intrigued by the spectacle, Antoine turned to talk to Jack, but he was gone. How does he keep disappearing like that?

Soon the players began to take their seats again, and there was Jack, sitting at the table opposite Tom's chair.

Tom was talking to some billionaire, drink in hand with his back to the table. He turned and sat down. As if he had been struck by lightning, he shuddered as he met Jack's eyes staring at him across the table.

Jack smiled and nodded. He calmly placed a stack of chips on the table, and the dealer began flipping out cards. The players' brows furrowed, and one by one, disgusted, they threw down their cards on the table. Jack looked serene. He smiled and stared intently at Tom.

Several hands later, Jack's stack of chips had grown substantially, and the other players' stacks were measurably smaller. Tom's demeanour had changed. He no longer looked like a victor. For a while, he looked defiant and determined. But now he looked annoyed. His evening had been spoiled. He was no longer in control, winning.

The other players looked bored. They were surely not bothered by losing a mere bagatelle. It just did not seem to be entertaining to them any more. They looked nervously over their shoulders, seeking an exit point. Jack kept smiling throughout, nodding softly as he picked up his cards, placed his bets, and looked Tom in the eye.

After a few more hands, Jack placed his fingers on the edge of the table, nodded in turn to each of the players, picked up several chips, and placed them in front of the dealer. He pushed his chair back, picked up his chips, and was gone.

By this time, Antoine had guzzled several more whiskey and sodas. He stumbled off his bar stool as he said out loud, 'Wow, he just disappeared again. How does he do that?'

Until then, he hadn't known that the two men knew each other. Tom had certainly seemed shocked to see Jack. I guess they were both seeing Ellie at the same time, he thought. Jack was around when I was with Ellie so why not? Maybe Jack has always been around Ellie.

Camille was as shocked as Tom to see Jack. What memories came flooding back to her. She had known from the beginning of their relationship that Tom would never be faithful to her. He was too rich to be worried by petty moralities. There were always going to be women who tried to bag him, and women he desired. He didn't think he had to try. He was Tom, and women would just fall for him – or so he thought.

She liked Jack. He had been a great lover, although as unfaithful as Tom. Their affair was only a brief fling, and had ended just before she met and married Tom.

But then Tom had discovered Ellie. It was as if Camille were a used carpet that could be rolled up and put away. He wanted to put her in storage while he had an open affair with Ellie.

When Tom found out that Jack was also seeing Ellie, he went into a rage. He didn't possess Ellie, but he wanted to. Then Ellie ditched him. He concocted all kinds of reasons to explain his loss. But he became convinced that it was Jack who had stolen her, right in front of him.

When Tom found out that Camille had been Jack's lover, he was livid. He didn't want his memory spoiled by the thought that she had been with that charlatan, Jack. From then on, it was as if Tom were torturing her, making her feel guilty about what had happened before she had even met him.

When Jack sat down at the table, she smiled at him, slouched in her chair, and felt relaxed. This was going to be interesting, she thought. When Tom sat back down and met Jack's eyes she thought he'd have a heart attack. Alas he didn't. He actually regained his composure rather well, she thought.

What is Jack up to? she wondered. He obviously has some scheme in process. He didn't come to play poker. Not even for the pleasure of taking some of Tom's money. Or maybe that was what he was after, money.

People thought Jack was rich. But she knew him from before he appeared on the scene as the new tech guru, when he was just a young grifter. He was calculating and didn't leave things to chance. Oh yes, he must be here to shake down old Tom. She was beginning to feel happier than she had been for a long time.

The next day Tom was furious with himself for letting Jack just walk in like that. How dare he show up at my table and fleece me and my friends? he thought. I should have had him thrown out, but I didn't want to cause a stir in the high rollers room. But I'll deal with that fraudster once and for all. He had better not show his face here again. But actually, I hope he does. My boys will take care of him. He had alerted the resort security, and all staff would be on the lookout for Jack.

Tom had decided he was going to see Ellie as soon as he heard she was booked to play the Volume. Of course he had to see her. He had sent a bouquet of flowers to her room. That was polite, he thought. She probably wasn't expecting that. She would have thought I would just show up. Well, I've changed, matured, he said to himself. But now Jack was back in the picture. Of course he was. He took Ellie from me the first time, and now he wants to stop me from having her again.

The past several months had been a busy time at the Galatian. The refurbishment of the Volume had cost a fortune, and there were the billions that the Metasphere was costing. The truth was, Tom needed cash flow, and lots of it. The casino had been chasing high rollers by offering them all kinds of incentives to come to the casino.

He had also relaxed the implementation of certain fiduciary rules. Oh, it will only be for a short time while I refill the coffers, he told himself. In the meantime, players with cash from all over the world had heard that the Galatian was the best place to move your money around at the moment. Cash, lots of it, had been flowing into the casino.

He thought, I have a lot on my plate. But tonight, I'm going to watch Ellie's show and see her backstage afterwards. He went to the Volume early, leaving Camille in their penthouse suite.

5

Ellie strode through the stage door and into her dressing room. A short while later, Abe came in looking for her.

'Hey Ellie I'm glad you're here … What the hell, is that you, Ellie?' He stood back to take in the sight.

She was wearing black footless tights, stiletto heels, a black leotard with bare arms with a high polo neck, and a purple mini skirt.

Her hair was short and blonde with ragged bangs down to her eyebrows, slightly teased for accentuation. Her bangs had been sprayed silver, and she was wearing large silver earrings.

Her face was pale with heavy black liner around her eyes and full dark eyebrows. Her eyelids were covered with white eye shadow and a dark purple line in the crease. She was wearing black mascara on her eyelashes and light pink lipstick.

'But Ellie, you've changed. What have you done?'

"I felt like a change. What do you think, Abe?"

'Ellie, all the billboards, publicity photos, the social media announcements, the videos, and the damned hologram all have you with long red hair, a flowing dress, red lips and nice country singer make up. That is your persona, and what everyone is expecting to see on stage tonight.'

'Yeah, well, I'm doing something different now. By the way, here is the new set list. Can you please give this to Antoine and the crew?' she said, handing Abe a sheet of paper.

Abe read it, muttering to himself. 'What are these songs? I don't know any of them. You can't perform these, whatever they are. You have to play your hits and stick to the agreed set list with two encores.'

'Oh, Abe, I'm not doing that anymore. I've had a change of heart, call it inspiration. Don't you worry, we're going to put on a great show.'

'Does Zachary know about this?'

'Why, of course he does, all the band are very enthusiastic.'

'Ellie, you get changed into your stage outfit, and put on a red wig. Quick, we don't have much time. You signed a contract ....'

'Are you going to tell me about the law, Abe? Are you going to threaten me or force me? Give it your best shot. I'm going on stage like this, and we are going to perform that set list.'

'What about your audience?'

'Maybe people will like what they see. Maybe they will like what they hear. Maybe I'm an artist, a musician with something to say, and maybe you should get on my side.'

Aghast, Abe turned and left the room and made his way up to the control box. 'Rodrigo, Ellie has had a breakdown, I think. Look, this is her new set list.'

'What? I don't know any of these songs. What about the lighting, the videos, the hologram? No, no, it's too late to make changes.'

Antoine grabbed the set list from Rodrigo and read it. 'Wait a minute, guys. I'll go talk to her,' he said.

He ran down the stairs to Ellie's dressing room. Ellie was sitting in a chair with her guitar on her knee, playing a song. 'Hi Antoine, you look out of breath.'

'Ellie, are you sure about all this? I mean, this could be bad for you. You're contracted to deliver a certain show, aren't you?'

'Do you like my hair, Antoine?'

In his excitement, he hadn't noticed that she had changed. He looked her up and down and said, 'You look sensational, babe. You really do, I love the silver hair.'

'Thank you, Antoine,' she said laughing, 'That's real nice of you to say so. I see you looked at the new set list?'

'Ellie, I don't think you can do this. I mean, the lighting, the videos, the hologram, they'll all be wrong, and I can't guarantee how the sound will be. I mean, what are these songs?'

'Antoine, I've been thinking too. I think that this is my show, my act. I don't have to do what you all tell me to do, this is my gig. Why won't anybody be on my side? All any of you want to do is use me.'

'Ellie, all right. You know I'll always support you and look after you, don't worry about me. Just so long as you know what you're doing.' He sat down on a chair with the set list in his hand, dumbfounded.

'Listen Antoine, you go and have a chat with Zachary. He and the band are all on board and ready to play. You tell that moron Rodrigo, that after the debacle of the rehearsal, I don't care if the lights, video and hologram are on, off or upside down. You tell him to be a professional and follow what the band and me are doing and light us appropriately.'

'OK Ellie, I'll tell him. Don't worry, the sound will be fine. I had reset it all anyhow.'

He smiled, what a move he thought. She sure came out fighting. 'Ellie, there's one thing I should tell you. I saw Jack in the casino.'

'Yeah, I know he's in town. He made himself known to me.'

'I also saw Tom.'

'Tom said he's coming to get me after the show. Jack will show up as well, no doubt. I don't want to see them, Antoine, I really don't. I don't know what I'll do, but I'm not going to run away from them. Will you help me, Antoine?'

'Ellie, I'll do anything for you. I love you. I've loved you since the moment I met you.'

'If you love me Antoine, then you protect me from everyone, look after me.'

Antoine walked back up to the control box and spoke to Abe and Rodrigo. He reassured them that the sound would be fine.

He said, 'Look, just light the stage and don't be too ambitious. All we have to do is pull this off tonight. We don't know about tomorrow's show, Ellie might change her mind and go back to the original plan.'

One by one, they abandoned the extras. Abe said, 'The hologram is bullshit anyway, the videos make no sense – a girl with red hair running through fields. Horses? Ditch it, ditch it all.'

Soon the audience poured into the Volume. They strained their necks, looking up and around at the amazing setup with the huge screens and hundreds of lights.

The lights dimmed, and Ellie and the band walked on stage to loud applause. She stood smiling until the audience quietened down. She said softly with her birdsong voice into the microphone, 'Hi y'all, it's great to be back in Las Vegas. I'd like to play you a song that I wrote. It's a love song titled 'When Will You be Loved.'

The song lilted through the Volume and the audience was silent. Antoine was very happy with the sound, but the lighting was flashing all over the room. He turned and shouted at Rodrigo, 'The lights look ridiculous – you're gilding the lily. Listen to the music, dig what she's playing.'

Then he felt and heard it again. Oh no, that damned drilling, it's going to ruin the show. He grabbed a roadie and sent him downstairs to tell him if the vibration and noise were bad in the auditorium. The roadie texted him ... 'It's not too bad, you can feel it but no one is noticing ...'

Ellie and the band played a set of love songs with a few rocking blues numbers. The audience was spellbound. You could have heard a pin drop in between the songs. Gradually the lighting was reduced until it was just a single spotlight on Ellie. Finally, Ellie played one of the most beautiful songs anyone had ever heard. It was about an angel that fell in love with a girl and lost his wings.

Antoine thought, Where did she get all these songs? Maybe she's about to record a new album. This must be the first audience to hear them. What a privilege.

She finished her song and came forward to take a bow. She called her band forward and introduced them. The audience seemed dazed; they started clapping slowly at first, but one by one they rose to their feet, and soon the whole auditorium was clapping and cheering. The crowd wanted more, more. Flowers and hats were thrown onto the stage. Eventually Ellie ran off stage, throwing her guitar to a roadie, but this time with a beaming smile on her face.

It was as if a great maestro had performed at La Scala in Milan. The audience would not stop. Encore, encore, they shouted, clapping in unison.

Antoine was amazed. That was the best performance I have ever seen in my life, Ellie darling, you touched the hearts of everyone here tonight, he thought.

The first one to make it to her dressing room was Abe. 'Ellie, you have to play an encore, three encores. The audience is going nuts, you can't leave them hanging, they love you.'

'Abe, I can't do an encore, I don't have anything more. You go tell them, tell them I've collapsed. I love them, but I have given my all.'

He left, and in the moment of solitude, her mood changed. Her racing heart slowed down, and she became calm. She knew what was coming next, and she was resolved, determined.

The door creaked, and Jack slid inside. 'Ellie, I'm so glad to see you girl.'

'You want me, Jack? You want to be with me again?'

'I love you Ellie. I'm your eternal lover, the one you'll never leave. We're twinned forever, you and me.'

'I know you love me Jack. I loved you too. I've missed you so,' she said.

Jack embraced her and she threw her arms around him. 'Ellie, come away with me tonight. I have a plane waiting.'

For a moment she forgot, as she always did, that Jack was a mirage, that she couldn't keep hold of him and that soon he would disappear again.

'Away, where will we go?' she asked. Jack smiled and half laughed, and his head dropped. His eyes turned to look directly into Ellie's, 'I know a few places,' he said.

Ellie didn't want to be under his spell anymore, she wanted to be free. She looked into Jack's eyes, and it came to her as a revelation – she didn't need him, he needed her.

Tom watched the show enraptured. As each song finished, he became more and more convinced that Ellie had written them about him. He thought, She's singing about us, about me! Did she want to perform here at the Volume because she knew I would be here to see her? My God, I must have her.

When Ellie ran off stage, Tom immediately stood up to leave, but the audience was crowding around, and he had to push his way through shouting, 'Get out of my way!'

When Tom left the penthouse, Camille thought, I know where he's going. This is the last time he will betray me. I'm through pretending, smiling sweetly and playing the part. I've been unhappy for so long, what does it matter now anyway?

She went to the Volume and watched the show from a seat high in the auditorium. She could see Tom, sitting in the VIP area. She watched him as he raised his arms and squeezed between everyone trying to get out. She made her way downstairs and out into the casino, past the gambling tables to the stage door.

Tom entered the room and saw Jack with his arms around Ellie. 'Ellie, you think you can choose Jack over me? You would really see him again in my hotel? You know I've always loved you. I'll always be there for you. We were meant to be Ellie, and after tonight's performance, I have to have you, you must be mine.'

Ellie reached into her purse almost involuntarily, like an animal defending itself, her fingers searching for the thing she had put inside.

Antoine came in to see Jack holding Ellie while she searched for something in her purse. Tom had his on hand on Jack's neck, and his other raised in a fist about to strike.

He shouted, 'Back off all of you!'

The three of them turned to look at him, frozen in place. Tom said, 'Who the hell are you?

Antoine picked up Ellie's guitar stand and shook it at Tom, 'I said, back off, I'm warning you!'

Jack shook his head and laughed. He let go of Ellie and moved a few steps backward.

Tom said, 'Me back off? This is my place, and my woman, why I'm going to ...'

Camille came in and said, 'Tom, you've betrayed me for the last time. I'll kill myself if you so much as touch Ellie.' She wanted to do at least one good deed in her life, and saving Ellie seemed like the best she could do.

They heard and felt a series of explosions like a strike of ten-pins going down. The lights went out and they were plunged into complete darkness.

Confused, Abe felt his way along the corridor to the dressing room in darkness, as sirens blared and the sounds of people shouting echoed through the Volume. As he reached the door and went in, the lights flickered back on.

'Ellie, the casino has been robbed, are you OK?' He stopped in his tracks. A man was lying on the floor, blood oozing from his body and a look of shock on his deathly white face, with a croupiers rake embedded in his neck.

Ellie stood still, staring down at Tom on the floor. Antoine, still holding the guitar stand, stood open-mouthed as if in mid-word. Camille looked shocked, all the blood drained from her face.

Out on Las Vegas Boulevard, crowds of people shuffled along, gazing up at the lights of the Bellagio and the Eiffel Tower. Further in the distance, the towers of the Forum, Mirage and Venetian hotels twinkled in the warm night air. Jack looked up at the sight and smiled. He sipped his drink through a straw and wandered along with the crowds until he disappeared into the night.

6

Antoine awoke to the barrage of chatter on the TV and felt safe, back in his environment, his home. He winced as he took a slurp of coffee, and his EV took him to the recording studio on Rampart Boulevard.

He was booked to play guitar on Ellie's new record. Ellie was in the vocal booth singing a pretty song as he walked in.

The producer spoke over the intercom from the mixing desk, 'Ellie, that's great, all we need.'

'What do you mean? I haven't even finished the song,' she said.

'Oh, that's all right, darlin'. We loaded the song into the AI engine. Don't worry, it'll do the rest.'

The producer noticed Antoine and said, 'Hey Antoine, it's your turn. You just play the first few bars on the guitar, and we'll take it from there.'

Antoine sat down on a chair with a guitar in front of him and several microphones arranged around. He checked the tuning of the guitar for a few moments, and then nodded to the producer, 'I'm good to go, you just say when.'

The producer said, 'All right, start playing.'

Antoine played for while, until the producer said, 'OK, that's great. You're done.'

'I haven't even got to the bridge, what do you mean 'done'?'

'Don't worry folks, the AI engine will take care of everything. You two go have a break, and we'll let you hear a rendition in a few minutes,' said the producer.

Ellie and Antoine looked at each other and shrugged. They went into the recreation area. It was set up with a bar and kitchen. Sofas lined the room, and there was a pool table in the middle. A large TV was mounted on the wall, with the news on and the sound turned down. Zachary and a couple of the band members were there lounging on sofas and watching the TV.

'Well, let's play a few frames,' Ellie said to Antoine with a half smile.

Antoine racked the balls and invited Ellie to break. She pushed the pool cue with surprising force, and the balls shot across the table.

One of the musicians turned up the sound on the TV and said, 'This is getting serious.'

Antoine lined up his cue, took a shot, and a ball sunk into a pocket. Ellie was leaning back against the wall with her fingers around the tip of the cue holding its base to the floor. She seemed relaxed in her black flowing dress, shoulder length red hair and red lips.

The TV flashed to an image of a burning truck heaped with bloodied bodies. A man ran in front of the camera, waving his hands, trying to make the camera turn away. But the camera kept steady. Men in hoods carrying weapons strode across the field of view. The sound of explosions and the whip-crack of gunfire burst out from the TV. The cameraman started to back away, still pointing his camera at the horrific scene.

As he backed away, the sky came into view, with drones hovering and buzzing. Flashes of fire emanated from the drones with smoke and deadly purple orange flames.

A rolling crawl of text flowed across the bottom of the screen ... the opposition forces have struck with overpowering speed ... the disputed president has fled the country ... hostages have been taken ...

Antoine took his next shot. Ellie looked distant, unaffected. 'Your shot, Ellie,' said Antoine. She smiled and moved towards the table.

The news moved to the next item with shaky video of a woman being hustled out of a courtroom. Her hands were bound in front of her, and her face turned towards the camera. She looked untroubled, almost satisfied. Ellie and Antoine both gasped in recognition.

The news reader said ... *Camille Diamon was sentenced for the slaying of her husband, billionaire Tom Diamon, who was killed on the night of the robbery of the Galatian Casino.*

The still unsolved robbery was possibly the biggest heist in history. In a brazen attack, the robbers drilled through the walls of the casino into the vault. An unknown amount of cash was taken, rumoured to be in the many millions of dollars. Multiple safety deposit boxes were blown open, and an unquantifiable amount of jewellery and bullion was also stolen. So far, the authorities have no idea who the thieves were ...

The producer came in and said, 'OK, folks. Why don't you come and have a listen?'

They crowded into the small studio, and the producer played Ellie's new hit song. Antoine, Ellie and the other musicians nodded in appreciation. It sounded great – nearly complete.

'OK guys, thanks. We can wrap it up now,' said the producer.

Antoine said, 'Wasn't this just the first session? I thought we'd be in here recording all week.'

'No, no, we only needed to get a few samples from you guys to make sure we had your voices and musical styles down pat. The AI engine will do the rest and we're done now. Thanks for taking the time to come in. Y'all enjoy the rest of your day.'

****

Sean De Siun spent his early years in Australia before moving to London in the early 1970s.

His written works include non fiction redactions, documentaries, screenplays and short stories. He currently lives with his wife in Sydney Australia.

Also by the author and available
from Art Camino Fiction

Avatara
Kings Road
Desire
Caanice and the Book
Katie
Chatter

Copy Sales
Available on **amazon.com**
Purchase direct from **artcamino.com/fiction**